"*I asked you what you were doing here?*"

"And I told you. Waiting for you." Nik's broad shoulders lifted in a shrug. "I knew it would not be long before you arrived to claim your inheritance."

His lips curled with contempt on the final word and she started violently. "How do you know about that?"

"Oh, you will find that news of such good fortune travels fast on Skiathos."

"I don't see that my inheritance has anything to do with you."

"On the contrary, Catherine, I think you will find it has a great deal to do with me."

REBECCA KING lives with her husband, two daughters and the latest in a long line of hamsters in an old redbrick house in an English village. She always wanted to be a writer, and worked as a journalist (including work on a tourist newspaper in Jamaica, where she lived for three years) and wrote children's stories before moving on to romance fiction. Researching locations for her books is the ideal excuse for her main interest—travel—and she unwinds by watching old black-and-white movies.

REBECCA KING

Passionate Inheritance

Harlequin Books

TORONTO • NEW YORK • LONDON
AMSTERDAM • PARIS • SYDNEY • HAMBURG
STOCKHOLM • ATHENS • TOKYO • MILAN
MADRID • WARSAW • BUDAPEST • AUCKLAND

For my father and mother.

ISBN 0-373-11814-7

PASSIONATE INHERITANCE

First North American Publication 1996.

CHAPTER ONE

THE key was not under the terracotta flower-pot where her grandfather had always kept it. She was still scrabbling for it when behind her she heard the door open. Jerking upright, she spun round and, screwing up her eyes against the late afternoon sun, she saw the dark outline of a figure in the shadowy doorway.

It was a man, she could make out that much—a tall, bulky shape. The caretaker maybe. And yet the ultra-precise letter from the lawyer in Skiathos Town had surely made no mention of a caretaker—or of any other man...

She gave a tentative smile. 'Er—*kalispéra.*'

No response.

Just for a moment fear stirred the tiny hairs on her nape, like an ice-cold finger. Who was he? A squatter? One of the freeloading 'sun, sand and anything else that's going' brigade that invaded the Greek islands each summer, who had seized the chance to move into the empty house and have a roof over his head for once? Perhaps...in which case, the sooner she put him right, the better. Squaring her shoulders, she went resolutely up the veranda steps.

'*Kalispéra,*' she repeated.

No response.

A flicker of anger ran through her now. Just who did this man think he was—and what did he think he was doing, arrogantly lounging in the doorway of *her* house? She ransacked her mind for the little Greek she could remember from that far-off summer. How on earth did you say, Do you speak English? Ah, yes.

'*Kséreté anghliká*?' And, when there was still no reply, she went on, her tone sharpening, 'What are you doing here?'

'Waiting for you, of course, Catherine. What else would I be doing?'

At the lazily spoken words, she drew in her breath with a little hiss. The voice was just as she remembered it—deep, sensuous, and with the vibrant warmth of all Greece in it—but with a new hint of caustic irony lurking just beneath the surface. A man's voice now, not a boy's.

'Nik?'

The single word was all she could frame from a throat all at once clenched strangle-tight, and as she stared at him he uncoiled himself with that same animal litheness which had so engraved itself on her mind, and sauntered across to where she stood, rigid with shock, at the top of the steps. Of all the people on the island of Skiathos she'd expected to see... Oh, come off it, her inner self cut in scathingly, all the way in the plane you *hoped*, didn't you? No, I did not, she retorted fiercely, and clenched her left hand until she felt the diamond solitaire in her engagement ring cut into her skin.

He was even taller than she remembered; he had to duck his head slightly beneath the overhanging vine branches, where the tiny bunches of green grapes were already forming. Taller—and the slim, youthful body had filled out now into that of a man, its strong, perfect lines enhanced rather than marred by the old black vest and faded denim shorts... And far more handsome—even more than in that dream which still sometimes returned, usually when she'd been feeling depressed or she and Julian had had a tiff—or rather, when *she'd* had a tiff, for Julian regarded rows of any sort as immature, somehow demeaning to himself. That dream, which after eight years could disturb her still, sleeping and waking...

He stood looking down at her as, thumbs jammed in his belt, he rocked slightly to and fro on the balls of his bare feet. Just for a moment she forced herself to meet the enigmatic gaze in those indigo-blue eyes she remembered so well, then her own hazel-green eyes flickered and fell, and she said, a trace more loudly than she had intended, 'I didn't know you'd be here.'

'Of course not.' The sardonic tone was surely mocking her. 'It is, nevertheless, a pleasant surprise, I'm sure.'

'A surprise, certainly,' she replied stiffly. 'But I asked you what you were doing here.'

'And I told you. Waiting for you.'

'But why?'

One broad shoulder lifted in a shrug. 'I knew it would not be long before you arrived to claim your—inheritance.'

His lips curled in open contempt on the final word and she started violently. 'How do you know about that?'

'Oh, you will find that news of such good fortune travels fast on Skiathos.'

His tone was even more barbed, and she retorted, 'I don't see that my *inheritance*, as you put it, has anything to do with you.'

'On the contrary, Catherine, I think you will find that it has a very great deal to do with me.'

Catherine stared up at him in bewilderment. Last time, Nik had *never* used this tone with her—never looked at her with such undisguised hostility. What on earth had happened in the last eight years to make him change? Or was it really her? Had *she* changed, so that now she saw people as they really were, instead of through a rosy adolescent haze? Maybe she was seeing the real Nik for the first time. She'd had a glimpse of it, perhaps, when he'd so heartlessly taken himself off that last afternoon without even a goodbye. But even so...

To try and cover her hurt, she said haughtily, 'You've no right to speak to me like this, but I'd be grateful if you'd tell me just what's going on.'

'If you really don't know, Catherine *mou*——' but he made not the slightest effort to mask his disbelief '—I shall be more than pleased to enlighten you.' He gestured with exaggerated courtesy towards the open door. 'Please—come in.'

Really, inviting her into her own house for all the world as though he owned the place! But she wasn't going to be thrown by him.

'Thank you,' she replied, and, putting her head in the air, stalked past him.

Inside, the sitting-room was just as she remembered it: comfortable, untidy, and with that faint mingled aroma of the huge pine-cones heaped on the wide stone window-sill, and tobacco smoke. Her grandfather's regiment of pipes was still arranged neatly beside the battered typewriter on which he'd tapped out his travel books.

She picked up a briar pipe and sniffed at it, and it was as if he had just put it down to go into another room. Clumsily, she replaced it and turned away, to see Nik watching her, still with that same unnerving expression on his face.

'I—didn't realise you knew my grandfather.'

'Oh, Gerald and I met. He was more a friend of my father's, though—a drinking friend,' he added sardonically.

'I see.' To avoid meeting those cold, watchful eyes, she glanced around the room again. 'It hasn't changed at all. Oh, except for that mirror.'

She pointed towards a huge gilt-framed mirror which hung on the far wall. Old, surely—its surface was slightly misty, and it reflected, gently, without the diamond brilliance of modern glass, the row of Chinese lacquer vases in front of it.

'He told me he found it in a bazaar in Istanbul—although it started life in a harem, apparently.'

'Really?' She gave a rather self-conscious laugh.

'Oh, yes. It was made to reflect beauty in everything it sees. Look.'

Before Catherine could draw back, he put his hands on her shoulders and steered her across the room, forcing her to stand in front of the mirror. In the subdued light from the half-closed wooden shutters an image shimmered back at her, casting a bloom on to her pale oval face, small delicate features and wide-set hazel eyes, and putting a sheen on her cream-fudge-coloured hair, which was neatly coiled into its usual immaculate chignon.

But she was barely conscious of herself, seeing only the image of the man standing so close behind her. At twenty, Nik had already had good looks in plenty; now, though, eight years on, he was, quite simply, devastating. His face was leaner, but this only revealed more clearly the classical bone-structure beneath the tanned skin. Now, it was a face of contradictions: hard—very hard—and yet an intense sensuality lurked in the thin mouth and in those steel-blue eyes, so thickly fringed with black lashes.

All she could see was his dark head, something cool—no, dangerous—lurking in his eyes; all she could feel was one bare thigh softly brushing hers, and the strength of his hands gripping her, the palms warm against her skin through the beige linen of her jacket; and all she could smell was the warm masculinity of the man, subtle yet insidious, winding itself around her like a potent spell. His presence filled her, so that her lungs swelled in panic until she could barely draw in air.

'An old mirror like this——' his breath stirred the hairs against her cheek '—is also supposed to see through the body to the truth within. What can you see deep within yourself, Catherine, I wonder?'

'I——' Half mesmerised by his voice, she stared into the eyes of her reflection, and for a fleeting second seemed to see something flicker across her face like the wind ruffling the surface of a pool.

At last he freed her, running his hands lightly down each side of her, into the curve of her waist and out over her slender hips.

'You've lost weight, Catherine *mou*,' he said softly.

She had to break the spell, the two of them caught together in the mirror's image.

'Lost my puppy fat, you mean, don't you?'

But the words came out jerkily as he took her hand, lifting it and turning it over to look at the fragile wrist where the delta of blue veins showed clearly beneath the pale skin. He rested his thumb for a moment against the pulse, and she felt it flutter then bound erratically.

'Anyway——' she snatched her hand away '—I've been ill. I had flu quite badly last winter.'

'And you have still not recovered?'

'Well—just about.' For some reason, though, her voice all at once sounded weak, as if she was still propped on her pillows in her London flat, sipping at a glucose drink, and as a sudden wave of dizziness washed through her she sank down abruptly into the nearest chair.

'Would you like a brandy? There's the odd bottle left in Gerald's cellar, I believe.' The ironic tone set her teeth on edge and she flushed.

'No, thank you. I'd prefer tea.'

'Ah, yes, I'd forgotten the English obsession with tea.' A brief, slanted smile. 'The cure-all for every stressful occasion.'

Catherine leaned back, eyes half closed, listening to the subdued sounds from the kitchen. He seemed very much at home, she thought with another twinge of resentment—and he still hadn't really explained what he was doing here...

As he set down the tray on a low wooden table, she said abruptly, 'Did you come here often to see him—my grandfather, I mean? You seem to know your way round.'

'I came here on occasions, yes. But I know my way round because I'm living here at present. Milk?'

'Yes, please.' The words came out automatically, but then, 'You——?' She stared at him, her eyes widening with shock. 'You *live* here? You mean...' she swallowed '...you're a sort of caretaker for me?'

But the thought of this man as anyone's caretaker was incongruous—and, as her own employee, downright unnerving. She'd pay him off—

right now—plus anything that her grandfather owed him. They were into May now, so with the tourist season starting he'd surely find another job very quickly. But, in any case, he had to go—now!

She drew in a steadying breath. Of course, she wasn't any longer the impressionable sixteen-year-old child—yes, child—that her sheltering parents had created and which was how he still clearly regarded her. She was a cool, sophisticated woman. But even so...

From beneath her lashes she slid him a quick sidelong glance and saw, as he reached forward to set her cup on the table beside her, a small silver medallion on a fine chain swing out from beneath the black vest. Surely that was the same St Christopher? He'd told her he'd been given it at his christening. That day, lying on the beach in the shade of the pines, running the fine creamy sand through their fingers, he'd unhooked it for her to look at and promised that he would buy her one, just like it. But that had been the last day, and he'd never come again...

Yes, he definitely had to go. After all, what would Julian say if he knew that her inheritance—an isolated villa over a mile from the nearest other habitation—brought with it a handsome Greek male, sporting a physique as superb as any one of those classical statues he so much admired? Though this classical statue was not cool marble, but warm flesh and blood...

Hastily, she picked up her cup, regarding him covertly over the brim. He was lounging back in the chair opposite, still giving every appearance of being far more at home than she was, and idly swirling a glass of ouzo until it turned milky white. Such beautiful hands, strong and supple...

'You must let me know how much I owe you,' she said stiffly.

'How much you *owe* me?' He raised his brows. 'In what way, Catherine?'

'Well——' he was putting her on the defensive again, and she went on in her best aspiring bank manager's voice '—I presume you've been looking after the house on my grandfather's instructions—or maybe his solicitor thought it advisable to employ you? Either way, if you will give me your account, I will——'

'I think, *koukla mou*,' he said softly, 'that you are under a misapprehension. Very slight, of course—and easily rectified.'

'Oh? And what's that?' She put down her cup and straightened slightly in the chair.

'You see, Catherine, the Villa Angelika belongs to me.'

She gaped at him. 'What on earth are you talking about? Of course it doesn't belong to you——' She broke off, but when he made no reply she went on, spelling out each word emphatically, 'This was my grandfather's house. He built it thirty years ago, and when he died he left it to me—his only grandchild—in his will.'

'I'm sorry to disabuse you,' all at once his voice was silky-smooth, 'but the will is invalid.'

'Invalid?' she echoed blankly.

'Precisely.'

He drained his glass and set it down with a decisive movement. Maybe he was drunk—although he hadn't until now shown the least sign of being intoxicated. Anyway, drunk or sober, it was time to put him right. Reaching for the bag at her feet, she fumbled through it and drew out a manila envelope.

'I have the will here, and a letter from my grandfather's solicitor.' She glanced down at it. 'Mr Joannides.'

He held out a lean, tanned hand. 'May I see them?'

Silently, she opened the envelope and passed the documents across to him.

'By the way, the will is a photocopy. The original is still lodged with Mr Joannides, so...' She left the sentence incomplete, but he grinned, a white-toothed wolf's smile.

'So I need not go to the trouble of destroying it?'

'Something like that,' she replied woodenly.

He glanced briefly at the papers, then looked back at her, his blue-black eyes basalt-hard.

'But you see, *koukla*, I have no need to destroy this will.' With a contemptuous gesture, he tossed it back into her lap.

'Oh, and why not?' she demanded.

'Because it is not worth the paper it is written on.'

'What?' Was he mad, or was she? 'Don't be so——'

'It is no use, Catherine.' His curt voice silenced her. 'I am afraid that in this particular game——'

'Game?' she broke in furiously. 'I'm not playing any——'

'I hold all the cards—including the ace.' From his shorts pocket, he pulled out a playing card and deliberately laid it face up on top of the will. 'The ace of spades.'

She gazed down at it with a curious sensation of foreboding.

'Well, so what?' she said, with as much assurance as she could muster. 'I——'

'Turn it over,' he said softly.

On its blue and white back, a few lines in Greek had been scribbled, and beneath that were three signatures—one in her grandfather's slanting hand—and a date—the February of the previous year. She stared down at that signature, her chill unease deepening, and when she looked up Nik was watching her over the arch of his fingers.

'What does it say?' With a tremendous effort, she kept every vestige of emotion out of her voice.

'That he consigns the Villa Angelika, its adjoining olive groves and beach, to Costas Demetrios.'

'Costas——?'

'My father.'

She shook her head in total bewilderment. 'But I don't understand.'

'I would have thought it was clear enough. My father is now the rightful owner of this house.'

'What?' She gaped at him in stunned horror, but then, faced with the implacable challenge in his cool, dark blue eyes, jabbed a finger at the card. 'Even supposing that thing says what you claim it does—and, of course, I have no way of knowing that, have I?' His dark brows snapped down threateningly, and she hurried on, 'Why write it on a playing card?'

'Because it was this very ace of spades which won my father the house.'

'And how precisely do you make that out?'

'I told you, he and Gerald were old friends. They spent most evenings together at the taverna talking, drinking—and playing cards. One night, when they'd both, I gather, been hitting the ouzo even more than usual, your grandfather suggested that they gamble each other's properties on the turn of a card. He suggested it—and he lost.'

There was a moment of total silence as she stared at him, her jaw sagging. Then, 'I don't believe you.'

He shrugged faintly and gestured towards the card. 'There is the proof.'

'A few illegible words on a crumpled scrap of cardboard?'

'Signed by the two principals and properly witnessed——' a tanned finger underlined the third signature '—by Michalis Tripou, a fellow customer at the taverna.'

'One of your father's drinking cronies, I suppose.'

'In that respect, he was more a companion of your grandfather's,' he replied coolly. 'And this card postdates that will of yours by six clear months.'

'What nonsense.' She managed a scornful laugh, hoping desperately that she sounded more confident than she felt. 'I must warn you, if you persist in this ridiculous claim, I shall contest it in the courts.'

'That's your privilege,' he replied levelly. 'One thing you should know, perhaps, is that next morning, when they had both sobered up, my father offered to forget the whole thing.'

'Oh, well, in that case——' relief flooded her '—there's no problem.'

'But your grandfather—acting out his part as a man of honour—refused. And, in that case,' he went on silkily, 'I am not my father.'

'Well, what's it to do with you, anyway?' She could feel the ground slipping away beneath her again and was fighting to keep a toehold. 'I'll go and see your father in the morning. He sounds as though he might be slightly less pigheaded than his son,' she added recklessly.

She saw Nik's fists bunch in his lap and his mouth compress until a thin white line edged it, but all he said was, 'My father has moved to Athens because of my mother's health, and he has put me in charge of his affairs on Skiathos.'

'Pity,' she muttered, but this time he chose not to hear.

'In spite of the wager, the two of them remained friends, and my father insisted that Gerald should spend the rest of his life here. The only thing that your grandfather promised in return was that he would change the terms of his will—a promise,' he added scathingly, 'that he obviously had no intention of keeping.'

Catherine's anger boiled over. '*If* he gave that promise, I'm sure he'd have kept it. And if he didn't, well—it must have been because he realised he'd been cheated—got drunk and then tricked into gambling with the—the local card-sharper.'

Her voice died to a gasp as Nik uncoiled himself from his chair. He stood over her, his thighs very near, the brief denim shorts so close-fitting that they sculpted the narrow pelvis and strong hips like a second skin. Below them, little dark hairs glinted against the sleek, tanned skin, and all at once, in spite of the terror of what her rash words had unleashed, she had to swallow down a sudden tightness in her throat.

'Catherine.'

He made no move to touch her, but at his tone she instinctively flinched back. For a second, she forced her eyes to meet his, winter-cold, but then looked down quickly to fix on the medallion at his throat.

'Y-yes?'

'I do not normally give people a second chance ... but you are foolish, and a foreigner, and have grown into a woman—of sorts.' She felt his eyes go contemptuously from her smoothly coiled hair to her neat navy linen business suit and low-heeled shoes. 'However, if you dare to impugn the honour of my family again, I shall——'

'Have me drummed off the island in disgrace, never to return, I suppose?' She tried to speak flippantly, but her voice was not quite steady.

'No.' Putting the side of his hand under her chin, he forced her face up inexorably to meet his arctic gaze. 'I shall—punish you myself.'

She stared into his eyes, impotent fury mingling with the fear inside her. Not once had he raised his voice, and the only weapon he had was a crumpled playing card—and yet she could feel all control of the situation slipping inexorably away from her. But she wouldn't allow herself to be intimidated by him.

'Really? I look forward to that.'

She threw him a defiant scowl, but then winced again as, for a moment, his thumb dug into the soft flesh of her chin. Finally he released her and leaned against the wall, jamming his hands into his shorts pockets as if to remove them from temptation.

Catherine sat for a moment, her lips pursed and her fingers tapping an uneven tattoo on the arm of her chair. Finally, she broke the fraught silence.

'There's only one way to settle this. I'm going back to Skiathos Town to see Mr Joannides—right now.' And catching hold of her bag, she got to her feet.

'But of course,' he agreed suavely. 'We shall both go, but——' he glanced down at the slim gold watch at his wrist '—not, I fear, this evening. Tomorrow we shall see him. I'm very sorry that you have had a wasted journey.' Though he hardly looked heartbroken.

'Not at all.' She set her head in the air. 'I'm afraid it is *you* who will be disappointed.'

'You think so?' The thin lips curled in a humourless smile, but then, as though all at once bored with the subject, he asked abruptly, 'How did you get here? A hire car?'

'No. I got a taxi from the airport.'

'I didn't see it.'

'I paid him off at the bottom of the hill.'

'Because you did not wish to share your first view of your inheritance with anyone else, I suppose.'

His tone was deliberately provocative but she refused to snap at the bait.

'Actually,' she said coldly, 'he didn't want to risk his suspension by coming any further up the track.' Although, in reality, Nik was half-right, at least. She had wanted to be alone, walking through the olive groves, reliving the magic of that summer. But this new Nik—so hard, so unfeeling—wouldn't understand that, would he?

'I see.' He studied her thoughtfully for a few seconds. 'I'm afraid Gerald stubbornly refused to have a telephone in the house, so I'll go down to the village and ring for another taxi for you.'

'What for?' she demanded truculently.

'Well, you will wish to find a room in Skiathos Town for the night—or a hotel. There are several good ones on the south coast.'

Their eyes met and locked, for a long, loaded moment, then without another word Catherine got up very deliberately, stalked out of the room, across the veranda and down the steps to where she had dumped her flight bag and case.

As she went to pick them up, she could hear Julian's voice in her ear—'Oh, darling, don't lower yourself to bandy words with such an unprincipled peasant'—and the temptation to turn and flee was all but overwhelming. But then, glancing up, she saw Nik lounging in the doorway again, his eyes coolly mocking, and her lips tightened. He was so— so arrogantly sure of himself, wasn't he? Taking a firm hold of her luggage, she walked back up the steps.

'Excuse me, please,' she said between her teeth.

But instead of politely leaping out of the way, he put up a hand to block her path. 'And just what do you think you're doing?'

'I don't know much about Greek laws—you do have laws out here, don't you?' she added sweetly, but, after one swift glance up into the coldly hostile navy eyes, kept her own fixed on his ribcage. 'But in England, possession is nine-tenths of the law. Sorry, but I have no intention—absolutely no intention whatever—of beating a retreat and leaving you with that nine-tenths. So, I'm staying.' And she butted his leg with her case.

He looked down at it for a moment, then straightened up. 'Very well. You can be my guest.'

'I am *not* your——'

'And I'll show you to your room.'

'Thank you, but there's no need,' she said tightly. 'I know the way.'

Taking a firmer grip on her cases, she marched back through the sitting-room and down the passage which led to her old room—the one which her grandfather had had built on for her, haphazardly, like all the various extensions to the house. She pushed open the door, but then stopped dead as, in one horrified glance, she took in the signs of male occupation—a crumpled shirt slung across the narrow bed, jeans draped over a chair, a pair of old black espadrilles.

Behind her, she heard Nik's lazy drawl. 'How delightful. I had not realised, *koukla*, that as well as moving into my house you would be sharing my bed.'

She groaned inwardly. In her agitation, she'd turned left instead of right—her old room was opposite. Hitching up her cases yet again, she swung round, feeling the peony blush sear her delicate skin.

'Sorry. My mistake,' she said through gritted teeth, and, pushing past him, opened the door facing her.

Yes, this was it. Her room, exactly as she remembered it—almost as if her grandfather had kept it specially for her. A painful little lump in her chest, she looked round at the small bed, the whitewood chest of drawers which Christos, the village carpenter, had made and painted with twining pink and white convolvulus flowers for her, the polished floor, with the beautiful faded Chinese rose-silk rug, which her grandfather had bought on a long-ago trip.

Everything was the same—except that in one corner someone had stacked a pile of canvases, half-finished oil paintings.

'Sorry about that. I'll move them.'

'So you still paint?' The words were out before she could hold them back.

'Of course. Well, I told you I wanted to be an artist eight years ago, didn't I?'

It was the first direct reference either of them had made to that other time; her eyes darkened with the memory, then slid downwards, unable to hold his direct, challenging gaze. His shoulders were smooth brown satin, with the faintest sheen of dark hairs, sloping to his throat, where a slow, strong pulse beat beneath the skin...

In spite of the soft breeze curling through the half-open shutters, the room felt all at once claustrophobic and, throwing her shoulder-bag down on to the bed, she said without looking at him, 'If you don't mind, I'll get some fresh air.'

'Have you eaten?' He was still blocking her way to the door so that she was trapped between him and the bed.

'I had lunch on the plane.'

'I said, have you eaten?' he repeated wryly.

'It was quite good, actually,' she replied tautly, still shaken by feelings she could not—dared not—analyse.

'You will join me for dinner.' It was a statement, not an invitation.

'Thank you, but no,' she said firmly. 'I shall go down to the taverna. Now—if you'll excuse me.'

He moved half an inch to one side, and, as she slid past him, her arm touched his. The tiny dark hairs brushed against her golden ones, making them prickle as if a low-voltage electric current was running through them. Without another glance at him, she walked down the passage and out of the house. Her arm was still tingling uncomfortably though, but only when she was safely out of sight did she dare to rub fiercely at it.

CHAPTER TWO

CATHERINE was halfway down the steep path before her flying footsteps slowed and she pulled up in the shade of a pine-tree with a rueful smile. She was an adult now—a sophisticated woman with a responsible job—and yet here she was, letting Nik Demetrios—funny, she'd never known his surname till now; all through that summer, he'd been just Nik—get at her, exactly as if she were still that young girl, trembling on the brink of—something, she hadn't known what.

It was just the flight, though, plus coming from a bitter English spring morning to the heat of a glorious Greek afternoon, and of course the shock of finding that Gramp's will was to be contested, that had done the damage—given her this strange, disorientated sensation. Nothing at all to do with *him*, she told herself fiercely and, half believing it, she went on.

But then, rounding a bend, she stopped again, a smile of astonished pleasure on her lips. Ahead of her was one of the small olive groves her grandfather had owned. The trees were ancient, their trunks grey and gnarled, but at her feet the grass was a drift of tall yellow daisies. Beyond the grove, the land levelled out to a meadow flowing with a sea of flowers: more daisies—white as well as yellow—scarlet poppies, purple orchids, the tiny mauve flowers of the wild sweet-pea, and a thousand cistus shrubs, their silky white petals drifting to the ground like confetti.

Last time there'd been nothing of this simple, heart-wrenching beauty, but that had been in the heat of summer when the grass had been brown and tinder-dry. She remembered the pines, though, bordering the meadow at the far side, and through them she glimpsed the unforgettable violet blue of the Aegean Sea.

The only sound was the wind rustling the silvery olive leaves and the soft shushing of the waves, and Catherine all at once felt burning tears sting her eyes. Was Julian right? she asked herself, chewing on her underlip. Or should such utter perfection remain just as it was for ever? Now, darling, you're becoming sentimental—that was what he'd say, of course, and shake his head, with that little smile of his . . .

The beach was just as she remembered it too: a crescent of creamy-white sand, fringed by the pines and sheltered at either end by low, rocky headlands. Although the sun had almost set, the sand still held the heat of the day so that it radiated up at her. She was horribly overdressed—and that was *his* fault, she thought resentfully, easing her clammy shoulders against her suit jacket. It had suddenly been so necessary to get away from him that she'd never thought of changing.

Now, unable to bear it a moment longer, she kicked off her shoes, unrolled her tights and dropped them beside the shoes, then looked round. There was no one here—it was a private beach, and the local fishermen kept away from it. Just occasionally, in summer, a boatload of young people would arrive and take possession, but her grandfather had always tolerated them unless, under the influence of too much ouzo and the strong resinated Greek wine, they had disturbed his writing.

After a moment's hesitation, she peeled off her linen jacket and camisole top, and finally stepped out of her skirt. In just her white slip, she went on down to the sea, her toes revelling in the powdery softness of the sand. The sea was cool, the water smoother than the silk of her slip, rippling as she walked up and down, and she felt the tranquil beauty of the place wind itself around her again.

This was where she'd first met Nik, and those magic days had begun. She'd been swimming and was just coming out of the water when she'd realised that someone was standing watching her, over by the pines. As she'd stood, her hand to her throat, he'd slowly come towards her and stood in silence looking down at her—even then, he'd been much taller than her—before introducing himself as Nik. She'd told him her name then solemnly put out her hand, and, with a crooked little smile, he'd taken it and they'd shaken hands...

A thin sliver of silver moon slid up now from behind the pines. She ought to go back. Reluctantly, she turned and saw, glimmering against the trees, something white. A split-second later, she realised that it was Nik, now in a white shirt. Just as on that other time, he was watching her, but he made no move to come to her. Something though— maybe his very stillness—was reaching out, binding her, drawing her to him. Whatever it was, she felt herself give a little jerk then, as if in a dream, start walking towards him, slowly, like a sleepwalker, never taking her eyes off him.

When she came up to him, she stopped a couple of paces away. His face was in the shadow cast by the pines so that his expression was unreadable. Then, very slowly, he raised his hands, took her by the shoulders, his palms warm against her bare flesh, and she went into his arms as if awakening from a century of sleep.

When she lifted her face, his breath curled against her skin and she felt the warmth of his lips against hers. Her own lips parted, but he made no attempt to probe deeper, only brushed his mouth to and fro across hers. The movement was very, very slow, yet there was something intensely sensual and erotic in the slight friction, something which quickened her blood and made every pulse in her body leap up in response.

There was honey on his lips, rich with the promise of endless nights spent lying in his arms... Even when she gave an inarticulate little cry and moved her shoulders restlessly under his hands, that slow, hypnotic movement never varied. It was as if he was asking a silent question of her, which her mouth and her whole body were answering. Yes, yes, yes. Oh, yes, Nik——

Her eyes, which had been half closed, fluttered then opened wide. What was she doing? What madness had gripped her?

Wrenching herself away, she brought up her hand, drawing the back of it across her mouth, scrubbing at it in a violent parody of his tender caress to wipe clean the honeyed taste as though it were deadly poison. She *never* reacted in this abandoned—*wanton*—way when Julian kissed her. She would, of course, once they were married—she'd told herself a hundred times that she'd have no inhibitions then. But that would be with her husband—the man she loved.

A single, intense shudder ran through her body, then she turned away, snatched up her scattered clothes and dragged them on. Finally, she caught up her shoes and tights and plunged blindly into the darkness of the pines.

He caught her up at the olive grove. 'Slow down, or you'll trip.'

On the surface, his voice was just as usual, but beneath the lazy drawl she caught an echo of something else—a sensuality which terrified her.

'No.'

But he took her by the wrist, holding her firmly as she tried to pull away, so that she was forced to walk stiffly beside him.

She ran the tip of her tongue around her lips, still throbbing slightly from his kiss. 'The flowers are beautiful. I—I hadn't realised.'

'Well, it was summer when you were here before.'

He spoke so matter-of-factly, she thought, with a little stab of pain. *When you were here before*... Those wonderful, totally innocent days—and evenings—when her grandfather had gone down to the taverna—when she and Nik had swum together, played beach-rounders with a piece of driftwood for a bat, and gone riding on his battered moped, she clinging precariously to his back, over tracks where no four-wheeled vehicle could travel.

Totally innocent... Oh, he'd kissed her sometimes then, but casual kisses dropped on to the top of her head as they splashed along the tideline, his arm draped easily across her shoulders... Except, that last afternoon...in the cool shade of the pines, she'd been tickling his nose with a blade of grass as he lay, hands behind his head, eyes closed. Suddenly the dark lashes had flickered, the blue-black eyes opened, and he'd stared straight up at her, as though seeing her for the very first time. Then, reaching up, he cupped her head, slowly drawing her down until her mouth met his.

The kiss was gentle at first, but swiftly deepened as his tongue parted her lips, to probe with a demanding, wholly new intensity. For a moment, she clung to him, yielding her mouth to him, but, as his grip on her shoulders tightened, she pulled away with a smothered gasp. His fingers held her just for a second longer, then he pushed her roughly away from him and rolled over on to his stomach.

He hadn't come next day, or the next day, or the next, even though he'd left her with his usual, 'See you.' For him, that time had been just an entertaining interlude with a naïve young English girl. No doubt, since then, almost drowned in the flood of women who pursued him, he'd forgotten all about her...

It was a strangely disagreeable thought, and to shut it out she replied coolly, 'Yes, of course. I should have realised—the flowers were all over then.' She stopped for a moment, breathing in deeply. 'What's that lovely smell?'

'Wild thyme.'

Dropping her hand, he went down on his haunches in the pale glimmer which was half daylight, half moonlight, filtering down through the latticed branches of the olives. When he straightened up, he took her hand again, his skin warm against hers.

'There you are.'

She felt the rough stems in her palm and, raising her hand to her nose, inhaled.

'You need to crush the flowers to release the scent of the oil.' His fingers closed round hers, and she caught the heady, pungent aroma.

'It's lovely—thank you,' she said stiltedly, but her skin was tingling once more from his touch.

'For me, it's the smell of Greece. If I were thrown down on to a hillside anywhere, blindfold, and caught that scent, I'd know I was home.' And, linking his fingers through hers, he led her on up the dark track, as sure-footed as a mountain goat.

On the veranda, he had lit small candle lamps on a table, which was laid for a meal for two. As she drew back, she felt the healthy anger stir in her, dispersing the drifts of emotion which clung to her like invisible mist.

'I told you,' she said tightly, 'I'm eating at the taverna.'

He spread his hands. 'But you see, *agape mou*, the taverna is not always open so early in the season—and I would hate you to have another wasted journey.'

'Well—actually, I'm not hungry.' All at once, the thought of the intimacy of a shared, candlelit meal was more than she could bear.

'Catherine——' his hands on her elbows, he forced her to face him '—I have prepared the meal, and you are going to eat it.'

'I've told you, I'm not——'

'If you wish, *koukla*, you shall choose all the topics of conversation—if that will make you feel safer with me.'

'I feel *perfectly* safe with you.' Though she didn't—not in the least.

'But of course you do.' Velvet-smooth, but she was quite sure that he knew the truth. 'So—please sit down.'

'I'll have to change—look.' She held up one slim bare foot, the sand still clinging to it.

He looked down at it with rather an odd expression on his face, then said absently, still with his eyes on that foot, 'You need not change. You look charming.'

He pulled out a chair, but as she dropped into it, he went on, 'Oh, just one thing——' And before she could protest, he deftly tugged off the navy elasticated circle which kept her heavy hair in a neat knot, sending it cascading to her shoulders.

'What did you do that for?' Crossly, she pushed it back behind her ears.

'Because I prefer it that way.'

While she was still searching for a fitting retort, he disappeared into the house and came back with a huge pottery dish of Greek salad, cold meats, one of the big country loaves which she remembered, and a bottle of chilled white wine. He set them down, then folded himself into the chair opposite her.

'Now, what do you wish to talk about, Catherine *mou*?' He was pouring wine into two glasses.

'How about—when you're going to move out of my house,' she demanded, her annoyance injecting a belligerent note into her voice.

'Oh, please.' He put his hand to his heart in a very Greek gesture. 'We have already exhausted that topic. Except perhaps, how long *you* plan to stay here?'

'I've taken two weeks' leave—quite long enough to sort this matter out, once and for all,' she added determinedly.

'Leave—from what?'

'I work in London—in a clearing bank.'

'Really?' He took a handful of blue-black olives. 'What position?'

'Well—I've just been made assistant accounts manager.'

'Congratulations.'

'Thank you. Julian says——'

'Ah, yes, the worthy Julian.'

Her left hand was resting on the table; he lifted it up and held it, looking down at the diamond ring. She couldn't see the expression in his eyes, for they were veiled by the black lashes which, in the mellow light from the candle lamps, threw a sooty shadow onto his hard-planed cheekbones. Even though she was willing herself not to react in any way, she must have moved involuntarily, for he glanced up at her then set down her hand.

'Tell me about Julian.'

'He's in banking too—that's how we met.'

'Ah, I see. So both of you are embarked on very—respectable careers.'

'Yes, we are.' She flared up instantly. 'And what's wrong with that? Let me tell you, it's better than—than just bumming around for the rest of your life.' She ended on a little gasp, but as he looked up at her again she was thankful to see no more than a flicker of ironic amusement in his navy eyes. 'I'm sorry. It's nothing to do with me,' she went on stiffly, 'but you were just trying to get at me, I know. And Julian is, well—doing very well.'

'Yes, of course, I remember Gerald telling me about him.'

She glanced at him warily, but his face was inscrutable. Her grandfather had come to England about eighteen months previously, partly for medical treatment, partly on a rather fraught duty visit to her father—the only child of a short-lived marriage. It had been marvellous to see him again, of course, but somehow she'd known, although he hadn't let slip a single word, that he wasn't happy about her choice of career. And she'd been uneasily aware too, that, even though he'd been extremely polite whenever Julian was around, he didn't in the least care for her choice of husband either. It had pained her deeply—and the thought of his confiding his misgivings to Nik was even more troubling.

'Julian's taken over his own branch since then—one of the youngest managers ever.' She knew she was starting to babble, but wanted desperately to keep talking about Julian, as if that would hold him there in the pool of candlelight between them. 'We used to work in the same branch, but he suggested I transfer—he thinks it's better if husbands and wives don't work together.'

'But of course.' Nik's tone was still deadpan, but even so she ransacked her mind desperately for another, safer, topic to carry them safely through the dangerous shoals of this cosy dinner for two.

'You still paint, then?'

His eyes glinted for a moment in the candlelight. With his needle-sharp awareness, he knew exactly what she was doing, but all he said was, 'As you have seen.'

'Did you do any formal training? I remember——' she stopped dead, then ploughed on resolutely '—you were talking about going to art school.'

'I did my training in Athens, yes,' he replied briefly.

'And who buys your paintings?'

'Oh, locals—and in summer I sell to wealthy tourists who use the yacht marina.'

'What sort of paintings do you do?'

He shrugged, as though tired of the whole subject. 'Landscapes, mainly. Portraits when I'm commissioned.'

'Portraits? Yes, I——' She broke off again, in even greater confusion. 'And landscapes—local scenes, you mean?'

'Sometimes.'

'I see.' Maybe she'd persuade Julian to buy a couple of views of Skiathos for their new house— although there was something faintly disturbing in the idea of having a part of Nik in their new home. Perhaps if he needed the money, though...

'And are you—successful?' she asked delicately.

Inexplicably, he grinned, showing those strong white teeth. 'Oh, I survive.'

Leaning forward, he sliced off some chunks of bread, speared one with the knife and held it out to her. 'Tell me, Catherine—purely as a matter of interest, of course—supposing I did not own the Villa Angelika——'

'Which you don't.' She snatched the bread, dropping it on to her plate.

'What were your plans for this place?'

She hesitated. 'Well——'

'Would you have come to live here on the island?'

'Of course not. How could I?'

'So you were going to use it as a holiday home?'

'Not exactly, no.' She was all at once very reluctant, under the penetrating gaze of those inky blue eyes which missed nothing, but then she thought, What the heck? It's nothing to do with you. 'Actually, we—Julian and I intend to finance a small tourist development here.'

'Really?' His tone was neutral. 'Do tell me about it.'

'Oh, nothing too large-scale, of course. I wouldn't want to spoil it.'

'Of course you wouldn't,' he agreed smoothly— too smoothly, although when she looked at him his face was unreadable in the soft candle-glow.

'But Julian thinks—that is, we think that a well-planned, low-rise scheme would be fine. A group of bungalow apartments, a small swimming pool, a tennis court——'

'And where were you aiming to put that?'

'Well, I'd thought of that level area below the olive grove.'

'In the middle of the flower meadow, you mean.'

'Yes, but now I've seen the flowers, obviously that's out of the question,' she replied tightly. He had made no real comment, and yet she could feel herself slithering on to the defensive again, and she didn't like it. 'We aren't philistines, you know. It would—*will* all be very tastefully done. Julian has a friend——'

'A friend? You amaze me.'

Her fingers tightened on the stem of her glass, but she fought down her temper. 'Julian has a friend,' she repeated icily, 'who is in the joint-ownership development business, and he——'

'Time-share, you mean?' Nik put in softly.

'Well yes, basically—but high-class. There won't be any touts in the streets of Skiathos doing a hard-sell, or anything like that. I insisted—I mean, we've agreed that already.' There she was, on the defensive again.

'You *have* set my mind at rest.'

'I'm so glad about that.' With surgical precision, she sliced through a piece of meat, then met his gaze full on. 'Look, it's obvious that you don't approve of our plans—not that it's anything to do with you—but can I remind you that it will bring employment to this part of the island?'

'On a limited, seasonal scale, maybe—while all the real money——' the temperature suddenly plummeted twenty degrees '—is siphoned off back to London to Julian and his—friend. You know, Catherine——' he shook his head '—you've changed. You have become a mercenary, greedy young woman.'

His words were like a dagger-blow to her heart and, wounded, she lashed out. 'Yes, of course I've changed. I'm eight years older—and the trouble with you, Nik, is that you haven't changed, and never will. You're going to spend all your life lying around in the sun, selling paintings when you can to tourists who've got more money than sense.' She wasn't going to buy any of his pictures, after all— he could live on bread and water for all she cared.

'You have also turned into a prissy, self-righteous little prig.' His words drove over her remorselessly. 'Gerald was right to be concerned about you——'

She winced inwardly. 'Well, he had no need, I assure you.'

'And to fear that you were becoming a carbon-copy of your parents.'

'Oh? And what's wrong with that?' she asked sharply.

'Plenty, according to your grandfather. He was bitterly disappointed in them—he thought they were a narrow, cold-blooded pair.'

'And did it ever occur to him that if my father is—well, very conventional, that could be a re-action to his own highly irresponsible lifestyle?'

'Yes, of course it did—though that didn't make it any easier for him to accept.' He paused. 'Your parents—they like your fiancé?'

She stared at him blankly for a moment, then her mouth tightened. 'Of course they do—they admire Julian enormously.'

His lips curled derisively. 'No doubt when you told them of your engagement, your father took you on one side and said, Catherine, my dear, here's a young man who's going to get to the top—you've made a very wise choice.'

'Not in so many words.' She jutted her chin stubbornly.

'Hmm.' He was leaning back in his chair, eyeing her in a way she did not at all care for. 'This development—it's all your precious fiancé's idea, isn't it?'

'No, of course it isn't,' she replied vehemently, but the guilty flush betrayed her.

'This place—doesn't it mean anything at all to you?'

'Of course it does.' Her voice was husky. How could he ask that? It was where she'd fallen headlong—desperately, painfully—in love, for the first time in her life. An adolescent crush, a holiday romance, she could see that now—nothing at all like the steady, feet-on-the-ground, but all the more permanent feelings she had for Julian—but no less agonising for that. And *surely* he must have known? Nowadays, she prided herself on masking her emotions; then, her face had been an open book, radiant with the adoration she'd felt for a handsome, teasing young god.

'Of course it does,' she repeated, more firmly. 'It's magic here. But you must surely see——'

'No. *You* must surely see——' his voice dropped into the warm air like broken shards of glass '—that any development, however—tastefully done,' savagely, he mimicked her, 'will destroy that magic forever.'

He drained his glass and set it down. 'Do you really expect me to surrender this lovely place so that your mercenary little boyfriend can despoil it?'

'Now look here.' Catherine's temper suddenly came to the boil and she banged her fists down on the table. 'I've had about enough of this. Julian is *not* mercenary. You don't know him—or my parents——'

'And have no wish to, either, when I see what they've done to you, between them.'

'You just keep your opinions to yourself.' She tossed her pale, fudge-coloured hair back. 'And, once and for all, this house is mine to do what I like with.'

'Oh, no, my sweet.' His thin smile was a million miles from his eyes. 'Let me tell you this—nothing I've ever done will give me greater satisfaction than to deprive the pair of you of this villa.'

'Oh, yes, it would really please you, I know.' She glared at him, her breast heaving. 'You—you've never done a real day's work in your life, this place drops into your lap like a—a ripe plum—and you're not going to give it up without a fight.'

'Too right I'm not.'

'Well, we'll just see what Mr Joannides says tomorrow, shall we, before you start counting your chickens?'

She stood up abruptly, sending her hair flying.

'Where the hell are you going?'

'To bed. I don't really care for the company.'

'The feeling's wholly mutual, I assure you.' His shouted words pursued her, echoing in her head even when she had banged her bedroom door to with shaking hands and leaned against it.

CHAPTER THREE

CATHERINE woke once in the night. She lay on her side, staring at the shutters, where tiny points of moonlight made a pattern of silver. Outside, the olives rustled gently, and down below endless little waves broke softly on to the beach. The sounds were hypnotic and, closing her eyes, she lay listening to them...

When she roused again it was daylight. She yawned and stretched, still half-asleep, then as she finally came to she rolled on to her back with a groan. Last night, she'd handled everything wrongly—utterly, totally wrongly. She'd been tired from the flight, of course, and then, coming face to face with Nik like that—this cold, implacable Nik—well, it had thrown her completely, splintering that smooth veneer she'd worked so hard on for years.

And the way she'd allowed him to kiss her on the beach, going unresistingly into his arms, as though the past eight years had just melted away... At the appalling memory, a scalding blush engulfed her whole body. But that, too, had only happened because of the effects of the journey, and nothing remotely like it was going to happen again. Otherwise, he'd get the idea that she'd surrender to him without a fight—and not just over the house...

When she'd stormed away from the table last night, she'd come in here, slammed the door, then stood motionless as a wave of panic took hold of her. She'd almost snatched up her luggage and fled, leaving the enemy victorious.

Almost, but not quite. And now, this morning—she sat up, hugging her knees, and scowled defiantly at the opposite wall—she was going to treat him exactly like one of the difficult customers facing her across her mahogany desk at the bank. She was going to be polite, ultra-cool, and *very* professional. Never again would Nik Demetrios be allowed to jolt her out of her composure.

What was he up to? She sat listening, but there was no sound. Still asleep—no doubt, his day never began much before midday. She'd wash and dress, then sneak—no, she wasn't sneaking anywhere—she'd *walk* down to the village and get one of the taxis which prowled up and down the only road on the island. That way, she'd beat him to the lawyer's doorstep.

Leaping out of bed, she caught up her toilet bag and cautiously opened her door. Still no sound. She was tiptoeing along the passage when, without warning, the bathroom door opened and Nik appeared, absolutely naked, apart from the small, low-slung towel he was casually knotting at his hip.

The shutters at the far end were still closed, making the passage dim, and for a moment he did not see her as she froze, one hand to her mouth. But perhaps he heard her faint gasp of shock, for he looked up sharply.

'*Kaliméra*, Catherine.' He smiled, showing those white, even teeth.

He must have showered. His chest still had a damp sheen, and there were beads of water gleaming in his black hair.

'I wish you wouldn't walk around like that.' The shock—and, beneath it, something else—put a brittle edge to her voice.

He came up to her and stood regarding her, taking in her neat, pink cotton nightie and sleep-tousled hair in a slow scrutiny which made her skin prickle, then finally he shook his head sadly.

'Tch, tch.' He clicked his tongue in reproof. 'Relax, *koukla*—you're as jumpy as a cat.'

'You *made* me jump.' That beautiful, satiny body was very close, so that all at once she couldn't breathe—couldn't think.

'Sorry about that.' He grinned unrepentantly. 'I'd forgotten for the moment that you were here.'

'Well, perhaps you'll kindly remember in future that I *am*,' she snapped.

He shook his head again. 'You know, my sweet, you really have grown up to be a Miss Prim and Proper. Let go—life's not that serious.'

One tanned hand came up to play with the white ribbon at her throat, and she felt the warmth of his fingers through the thin cotton. That light touch was having a strange, disturbing effect on her, making her whole body feel hot yet at the same time shivery, while her blood was beginning to pound in her ears. Somehow she pulled herself away.

'I happen to think it *is* serious—and it's a pity that you don't feel the same. You might even make something of yourself.'

'You think so? Poor Catherine.' His lazy voice mocked her, though the blue-black eyes were unreadable. 'And poor—what was his name? Oh, yes—Julian.'

'Just what do you mean by that?'

'Nothing—I'm sure you will be perfect for each other.'

Her fingers bit into her toilet bag until she heard the popper burst.

'Yes, we shall,' she said through her teeth and, head in air, went past him, crashing the bathroom door behind her.

But then she leaned up against it, her face screwing up, half angry, half horrified. Five minutes—that was all it had taken, and her resolution to treat him with the icy disdain he deserved lay in shards at her feet on the tiled floor. Instead of abusing her inoffensive toilet bag, what she'd really been longing to do was launch herself at him, fists flying, and wipe that cool, sneering smile off his lips once and for all.

She caught sight of herself in the mirror and blew out a furious breath. If Julian could see her now, he wouldn't recognise her—face flushed, hazel eyes blazing like a ruffled, spitting cat's, breasts still heaving under the storm of anger. Strangely subdued, she stripped off her nightdress and set the shower running . . .

Nik, still stripped to the waistband of his denim shorts and apparently absorbed in a sheaf of papers, was just finishing his breakfast when she appeared on the veranda. He swept the papers up and dropped them into an attaché case by his side.

'Coffee?'

'Yes, please.'

She watched as he filled her cup, then refilled his own.

'Black or white?'

'White, please.'

He pushed a blue pottery jug across to her. 'Try this milk—it's from my own goats.'

When she looked up at him in surprise, he went on, 'I've bought a couple to keep up on the hills behind the house—they spend their whole lives there. I'm quite sure you can taste the flowers in their milk.'

She gaped at him. 'You've milked them—this morning, I mean?'

'Of course. I looked in on you to see if you wanted to join me, but you were still getting your beauty sleep.'

He spoke carelessly, but the thought of Nik, seeing her while she slept, relaxed and defenceless, was strangely unnerving.

'You must have some yogurt, too—courtesy of Ariadne and Persephone, as well.'

'Ariadne and—— The goats, you mean?'

'Of course—and very fetching ones, too. Long, silky cream coats and bells round their necks.'

In spite of her fraught nerve ends, she laughed out loud.

He quirked a black brow. 'What's the matter?'

'Oh, nothing,' she said hastily. 'I was just thinking what a romantic you are.'

'And in your book——' Suddenly his dark eyes were chisel-hard '—I suppose that's nothing short of a crime.'

'Oh, no—no, of course not. It's just——' she was floundering with embarrassment '—well, you're so dynamic, so full of energy. If you could only channel it sensibly, you could do anything.'

'Sensibly? Hmm.' He pursed his lips. 'But Catherine, perhaps I don't want to *do* anything!'

'Well, that's up to you,' she muttered. 'It makes no difference to me whether you choose to make anything of your life.' And, neatly splitting a bread roll, she buttered it and began eating in silence.

When she had finished, she began gathering the dirty crockery together.

'Leave that.' Nik jumped to his feet. 'Are you ready?'

No chance now of getting to Mr Joannides alone... She smoothed down the skirt of her navy voile dress and picked up her bag. 'Yes.'

'OK.' He glanced at his wristwatch—slim, gold—
a Rolex? Surely not—although that was just the
sort of extravagance he'd squander any money on
that happened to come his way. 'Right, let's go.'

'But——' she stared at him round-eyed '—aren't
you going to—well——?' Her eyes slid away from
that powerful torso.

'Sorry.' He grinned. 'I forgot.'

A scarlet T-shirt hung from the back of his chair.
As he tugged it down over his head it ruffled his
hair, so that a black lock fell forward over his brow.
All at once, Catherine had an almost irresistible
urge to run her fingers through it, to neaten it, and
she tore her gaze away again as he thrust his feet
into a pair of shabby trainers.

'But surely you're going to change?'

'What into—a salamander?' Nik asked over his
shoulder.

'No, of course not.' He was playing with her
again, and it annoyed her. 'Into suitable clothes for
seeing my lawyer.'

He threw back his head in a sudden laugh, ex-
posing the strong column of his throat. 'Catherine
mou, this isn't London or Paris, you know.'

'Yes, but——'

'So what do you consider suitable clothes for a
visit to *your* lawyer?' Suddenly, he seized hold of
her by the wrist. 'Come and choose for me.' And
before she could argue, he had whisked her into
his bedroom.

The bed was still rumpled, a dent in the pillow where his dark head had lain all night. No pyjamas, of course—— She jerked her eyes away as, with a dramatic flourish, Nik flung open his wardrobe door.

'It's all yours.'

He was standing just behind her, so that she could smell soap and aftershave, but beneath that she caught another faint scent which at first she did not recognise. Then she realised with a jolt of her senses that it was the scent of Nik, the man himself—warm, vibrant, and intensely masculine. Funny, she'd never once been conscious of that with Julian. Horrified by the disloyal thought, she put her hand up and began running it rapidly along the rack of garments.

No suit, of course. Well, she could hardly have expected that, could she? Nik, sleek in a charcoal-grey suit...white silk shirt...discreet tie—the very thought was so incongruous that her lips twitched. But then, as the full force of the image she had conjured up struck her, her breath caught in her throat.

'Well——' behind her, she heard his lazy drawl '—do you really want me to go in those?'

Realising that her hand had tightened on a pair of cut-off jeans, she said hastily, 'No. These, I think.'

Without looking at him, she brought out a pale-blue cotton shirt and a pair of white canvas trousers and passed them to him. But then, as he dropped them on to the bed and put a casual hand to the zip of his shorts, she fled back to the veranda.

When he emerged a couple of minutes later, she was intently studying a couple of tiny green lizards, basking at the top of the steps in the early morning sunshine.

'Ready?'

'Of course.' She picked up her bag again. 'Shall we get a taxi in the village?'

'No need. I'm taking you in myself.' And he dangled a set of keys in front of her.

So, at least he'd given in to the proprieties sufficiently to buy a car. She followed him round to the back of the house, stood while he slid back a door of one of the ramshackle outhouses—and then gave an almost audible groan.

Standing inside was not a car, but a huge, powerful-looking motorbike. When Nik wheeled it out and propped it up, the sunlight winking on its black and silver frame, it looked even more formidable. He swung his leg astride and inserted the key into the ignition.

'Get on, then.'

'But I——' She was having problems with her voice again. 'No, I'll walk down—get a cab.'

Nik straightened up and, gripping the wide handlebars, looked at her.

'You will get on—right now,' he said grimly. 'For heaven's sake, Catherine, what is wrong with you? You rode on my moped happily enough last time, didn't you?'

'Yes, but that was—last time,' she replied, frozen-faced.

She was remembering their first ride. It had been a lovely evening, warm and drowsy, the trees casting long shadows across their faces as they'd ridden up the steep, winding hill to that old monastery. It had been cool inside the tiny white church, the little lamps flickering in front of the altar, the air sweet with the scent of roses around the picture of the Virgin. Then, outside, they'd sat under the vines, drinking lemonade and watching as the sun went down behind the far mountains, in what she was quite sure must have been the most beautiful sunset ever since the world began.

They'd ridden slowly back, her cheek against Nik's back as she clung tightly to him, as if she could never bear to let him go. Oh, God! Her eyes closed as she felt a vestige of the bitter-sweet pain of that other time reach across to her, entrapping her, then fiercely she shook herself free of its spell.

She turned to head off down the track, but Nik's voice halted her. 'Catherine—if you don't get on——' he rolled the bike alongside, so that the front wheel brushed her leg '—I shall follow you—on this—all the way down the hill, then forbid any taxi driver to pick you up. I shall tell them it is a lovers' quarrel.'

She stood irresolute for a long moment, then, without looking at him, hitched up her dress and climbed on behind him. As she sat stiffly upright, he switched on the ignition, the machine gunned into life, and Catherine, her eyes wide with sudden terror, just had time to clutch him round the waist as they roared off, bumping down the dusty, rutted track.

A flock of placidly grazing goats leapt for their lives, and then they were down on the road, flying past white-painted villas and holiday apartments, smothered in climbing roses and creepers. The wind tugged at her hair, tearing it free of its pins, and snatched at her skirt whilst the blue Aegean flashed past alongside. When he finally pulled up in a side street near the centre of Skiathos Town, she was laughing from the sheer, crazy exhilaration.

As she climbed off, she looked up at him still laughing, and pushed her tangled hair off her face.

'That was really great.'

The words came out before she could prevent them, but for once Nik did not give her that lazy, mocking smile or make some cutting remark. He only stood, holding the keys and staring down into her upturned face.

Then, after an endless time, he said, 'You've got some dust on your cheek. Keep still.'

His thumb brushed the side of her face, then he turned away...

'Ah, Miss Turner. How do you do?' The lawyer— younger than she had expected—came from behind his desk and they shook hands. 'May I say how sorry I was about your grandfather? He was an amazing man. I count it a privilege to have known him.'

'Thank you.' She smiled warmly. 'I'll tell Dad what you said.' She wouldn't, though. Unsolicited testimonials from fifty foreign lawyers wouldn't alter her parents' opinion of Gramps...

'Nik!'

'Stavros!'

Catherine, just lowering herself into one of the leather armchairs, stared in astonishment as the two men, after formally shaking hands, clasped each other in exuberant bear hugs. Nik? Stavros...?

They were well launched into a flow of lively conversation when Nik caught her eye.

'Oh, I forgot. We must speak English—Miss Turner does not speak Greek.'

No, she doesn't, Catherine thought spikily, behind another polite smile.

'I'm so sorry, Miss Turner, it was most ill-mannered of me,' the lawyer said smoothly, then turned back to Nik. 'And how is your mother?'

'Much better—responding well to treatment. And Christina—she's well, I hope?'

'Radiant. Couldn't be better.'

'When is the baby due?'

'In three weeks. But——' his broad smile included her '—you know babies, Miss Turner. They come when they're ready.'

Catherine, her nerves drawn out to squeaking point, suddenly could not stand any more. 'I gather you two know each other,' she said stiffly.

Nik sank down into the chair beside her. 'We were at school together.'

She felt her stomach lurch a fraction. How naïve she'd been. In a tiny island like Skiathos, of course everyone was going to know everyone else. And then another thought struck her, a thought which had been niggling in the back of her mind since the previous day. Nik had known that she was coming—he'd told her that. So, in that case, could he possibly have been tipped off by an old schoolfriend?

She set her bag down at her feet then, as the lawyer seated himself behind his desk, said, 'Mr Joannides, I hope you won't misunderstand me, but can we clear up one thing straight away? I know you were my grandfather's solicitor, but just who are you acting for in this matter? Whose interests do you serve—mine, or those of Mr Demetrios?'

From behind his rimless spectacles, he gave her a level look. 'The interests of justice, I should hope, Miss Turner.'

A lawyer's answer, if ever she'd heard one. Well, she wasn't going to be intimidated. Even so, she shot Nik a sideways glance and was chagrined to see that he was lounging back in his chair, wholly at his ease. *She* was sitting bolt upright, tense and on edge, while he—any minute now he'd have his feet up on the table.

Ignoring him, she turned back to the lawyer, putting on her most crisply efficient businesswoman's tone. 'But are you also Mr

Demetrios's solicitor? If that is the case, I really think it would be better—less embarrassing for you both——' though neither of them looked particularly embarrassed; rather, they were exuding an infuriating impression of two Greek males effortlessly ganging up on a mere woman '—if I put *my* affairs in the hands of someone else.'

'Oh, but I assure you, Miss Turner, that since moving to the mainland Mr Demetrios Senior has employed the services of a lawyer in Athens. And as for Mr Demetrios Junior—well——' he flashed Nik a sideways smile '—I don't think lawyers feature very high in his priorities. And besides, the mere fact that, for years, he consistently beat me— and everyone else, for that matter—in academic work, in sport, in success with the girls——' the two men exchanged another glance which set Catherine's teeth on edge '—will not be allowed to colour my professional judgement in the slightest.'

She nodded briefly. 'Very well.'

'Now——' he reached across for some papers, including, she realised, the original of her grandfather's will '—the essential problem is to establish legal title to the house, the surrounding land, and the beach beyond.'

'But surely there *isn't* any problem,' she pointed out in her most reasonable tone. 'After all, it was *my* grandfather who bought the land and built the house on it, so——'

'Of course,' he agreed placatingly. 'But we also have the unfortunate matter of the wager.'

'Yes, but can you really establish—what did you call it?—legal title with a tatty old playing card?'

She shot Nik another glance from under her lashes; he was leaning back, looking ever so slightly bored.

'A nice point, Miss Turner. A properly executed and witnessed will—I drew it up myself—set against a playing card, also signed, dated and witnessed.' The lawyer pursed his lips. 'I have consulted my uncle, who is a member of the judiciary in Athens, and he referred me to the precedent of——' he flicked through his notes '—Panayotopoulou versus Vasiliades—a case with some similarities, except that there a restaurant menu featured instead of a playing card and a woman, who in her time had been mistress to both the main parties, was one of the plaintiffs.'

'And who won?' she demanded impatiently.

'Ah, well,' he shook his head, with a faint smile, 'that is another legal nicety.'

'You mean nobody won—except the lawyers,' drawled Nik.

Catherine chewed her lip in frustration. She really didn't want to get involved in an expensive lawsuit, which could possibly drag on for years. On the other hand, why should she tamely hand over the villa without at least putting up a fight for it—as, surely, her grandfather had intended? Despite Mr Joannides' soothing words though, she still felt so horribly alone. If only Julian were here to help, advise her what to do even . . .

'Well, Catherine——' for the first time, Nik looked directly at her '—what do you think? Or rather, what would Julian think?'

In her lap, her hands clenched together. Was he a mind-reader on top of everything else? 'You can leave Julian out of this,' she muttered.

'But does *he* want to be left out?' he enquired silkily, then turned to the lawyer. 'Miss Turner's fiancé was intending to turn the Villa Angelika into a time-share complex.'

'Well, there is a great deal of development going on in Skiathos,' Mr Joannides responded diplomatically. 'And much of it by foreigners.'

One particular foreigner tapped her fingers on the side of her chair. 'Tell me, Mr Joannides, have you any knowledge of my grandfather's making a later will, or having any intention of changing his existing one?'

'To the best of my knowledge, no,' he replied cautiously. 'He certainly had not intimated as much to me.'

'Well, surely that settles it, then.'

'Except that the card, which I hold, postdates any will of yours.' Nik's indolent tone did not wholly mask the thread of steel, but she spoke directly to the lawyer again.

'So, what do you suggest, Mr Joannides?'

He looked from her slightly flushed face to Nik's expressionless one. 'I suggest you both try to reach an amicable agreement, without resorting to litigation.'

Catherine gave a brittle laugh. 'But that's quite impossible. After all, the only amicable agreement Mr Demetrios will accept——' she flashed him a nasty look '—is one where I retreat to England, this morning if not sooner, and leave him in sole, undisputed possession. Well, I'm sorry, but I don't intend to do that.'

She jutted her small chin pugnaciously, and the lawyer regarded her thoughtfully, the faintest gleam in his brown eyes.

'No, I must say I do not see you retreating easily, Miss Turner. So in that case, perhaps you would consider making Mr Demetrios a fair offer for his claim.'

'Absolutely not.'

'I most certainly will not.'

They both spoke together, glaring at each other, but then Catherine all at once had had enough. Abruptly, she got to her feet and stood looking down at the lawyer.

'Thank you for your advice, Mr Joannides, but I'm not a quitter. My grandfather was obviously ch——' she caught sight of the sudden flash of cold fire in Nik's dark blue eyes and, her courage failing, went on instead '—he clearly intended me to have the house, so I shall do all in my power to carry out his wishes. No doubt we shall be in touch again very soon.'

And holding out a firm hand, which he took, she turned sharply on her heel and swept out of the office.

CHAPTER FOUR

She was standing in the street, still trying to make up her mind which way to go, when Nik came clattering down the stairs.

'Well?' he demanded. 'Satisfied?'

'Not really. We're no further on.'

'But at least we know where we stand.'

A car swept round the corner, much too fast, and Nik snatched her up on to the pavement then yelled something highly unpleasant-sounding after the driver.

'Don't *do* that!' she hissed.

'Don't do what?'

'Make an exhibition of yourself—and me.'

'Why not?' He grinned down at her unrepentantly. 'It's one of the small pleasures of life. I've told you, *ghatakhi*—relax. Come on, let's go.'

But she barely heard him. *Ghatakhi* . . . kitten. That was what he'd called her that other time. He'd told her she wasn't old enough to be a Cat—just Kitten, and then he'd smiled and gently tapped the end of her nose . . .

She was astonished to find intense sadness welling up in her and, to cover her inner turmoil, said waspishly, 'I'm surprised you didn't push me under it.'

He gave her a slow smile. 'You underestimate me, *koukla*. That would be too easy. I like a fight—especially with a beautiful woman—and particularly if I am sure of the outcome.'

'And you're so sure of the outcome—so confident that you'll get the villa?'

'The villa? Oh, yes—of course. But I wasn't in this case thinking of the villa.'

At the unmistakable meaning in his eyes, Catherine felt the sudden colour blaze in her cheeks. Hitching her bag up on to her shoulder, she swung away, but he caught her by the arm.

'Where are you off to now?'

'Back to the house. I'll get a taxi.'

'Now don't go buttoning up again.' Nik looked down at her reprovingly. 'You loved that ride into town.'

'Maybe, but——'

'And you know I'm a very good rider.' As she stood, scuffing a pebble at her feet, he put his hand under her chin, tilting her face to his. 'So—you're perfectly safe with me.'

Am I? The words almost bubbled from her lips, but she caught them back just in time. A grey taxi was cruising past and she took a step towards it, but Nik grabbed hold of her again, gesturing the driver on.

He towed her along Papadiamantis Street, then down a quieter, narrow alley and only released her when he turned into what was clearly an art gallery. It was simply furnished, with whitewashed walls and rush matting, the only colour provided by the paintings on the walls. A middle-aged man appeared through a bamboo-bead curtain and greeted Nik. They were saying something about her—she knew that, for the man smiled politely and nodded at her, his eyes frankly curious, but then he drew Nik away to the far end, leaving her to wander.

A few of the paintings were in delicate watercolours but most were executed in oils. She made her way along them, taking in the seascapes, fishing boats and white-painted houses, but then she halted abruptly in front of one painting. It was quite different from the rest, its subject not Skiathos but a desert.

Under an intense, burning orange sky lay a range of low-rounded hills, not painted so much as sketched in rapid lines, and in the foreground the sand blazed red-gold. The painting was like fire— it almost scorched her, the heat coming out at her in waves so that she half-expected to see little flames licking round the frame.

She stood rapt for several minutes before becoming aware of Nik standing beside her.

'Do you like it?'

'Yes, it's marvellous. Do you think they'd take a credit card? It would make a wonderful——'

When she broke off abruptly, he raised his brows in polite enquiry. 'A wonderful——?'

'Wedding present for Julian,' she went on, more constrainedly.

'I don't somehow think that Julian would care for that painting,' he said curtly.

'Why not?' she demanded. 'I've told you—you don't know him.'

He gave an infinitesimal shrug. 'In any case, the painting is sold.'

'It doesn't say "Sold",' she said stubbornly, gesturing to several other pictures, each with discreet red stickers on their frames. 'I'm going to ask.'

'Catherine.' He put his hand around her waist, pulling her round so sharply that she had to fling up both hands to avoid being crushed to his chest. 'The painting *is* sold.' And he held up a huge wad of bank notes.

She looked from them to him, then swallowed and said, almost fearfully, 'You mean—you painted it?'

'That's right.' He tapped the bottom right hand corner, and for the first time she saw the N.D. in bold black lines.

'Do you know who's bought it?'

'Oh,' another lazy twitch of the shoulder, 'a German industrialist who's just brought his yacht into the marina—you know, one of those tourists with more money than sense you were telling me about.'

Her lips tightened slightly as the thrust struck home, but he went on suavely, 'You know, *koukla mou*, I think there may still be hope for you, after all.'

'And what's that supposed to mean?'

'Simply that you seem so—cool, so much on your dignity. And yet, for you to be drawn to this painting, which is all fire and heat, reveals that that side of you—which I was beginning to think I had imagined—does still exist.'

'Yes, well—maybe I don't like it quite so much now I look at it again,' she snapped.

'Does still exist, deep down but not entirely smothered, even though—certain people have done their best to do so,' he went on inexorably, 'and lies waiting for the right man to rekindle it.'

'Stop it,' she blurted out. 'You're not to talk to me like that.'

'Indeed?' A quirk of his black brows, then with a casual '*Andio*' to the gallery owner who was watching with open interest, he propelled her outside.

Next door was a small jeweller's shop, and Nik brought her to a halt alongside the window.

'I seem to remember—a long time ago—promising to buy you a bracelet.'

'Oh, no—please.' Embarrassment that he might be going to spend money on her struggled with the treacherous pleasure that he had remembered. Embarrassment won. 'I really would rather you didn't.'

'Nonsense,' he said calmly, and flourished the notes at her. 'These are burning a hole in my pocket.'

Next moment, her feet were over the doorstep and she was standing on the cool, tiled floor. As a young man came forward—greeting Nik like a long-lost brother, of course—her eye fell gratefully on a tray of pretty little Greek-key bracelets, only a few hundred drachmas each.

So when Nik turned to her and said, 'Now, Catherine, do you see anything you like?' she pointed firmly to the tray.

'Those bracelets are very nice.'

But as the assistant moved towards them, Nik waved an imperious hand and said something in Greek. She really would have to learn this appallingly difficult language if she was going to be spending much time in his company—it was too dangerous not to know what was going on.

Discreetly positioned at the rear of the shop was a tall wooden cabinet, and the young man unlocked one of the drawers, brought out a shallow box and set it on the counter. Half a dozen silver bracelets lay in a bed of cotton wool; Nik surveyed them swiftly, then took out the largest one.

'Hold out your arm.'

And Catherine, after a private, mutinous glance up at him, obeyed, allowing him to slide the bracelet into place. It was of heavy, antique silver, inset with huge turquoises in silver inlay, and very wide, so that it enhanced the slender bones of her wrist.

'Please,' she began in an urgent whisper. 'I'd rather have——'

But he was already turning to the man. '*Tha to paro tora.*' And she was forced to watch in smouldering silence as a bulging pile of bank notes was transferred from one side of the counter to the other.

Outside, she swung round on him furiously. 'You shouldn't have done that. You—you're impossible.'

'Don't you like it?'

She looked down at the bracelet, her thumb gently smoothing across one of the blue-green inlays.

'Yes, of course I do. It's beautiful—really beautiful. Thank you, Nik,' she said huskily, but then, because the silly lump in her throat made her angry with herself now, 'You shouldn't have bought it, though. You'll never have any money if you keep squandering it all the time. That watch——'

He glanced down at it carelessly. 'What about it?'

'It's a Rolex, isn't it?'

'Could be.'

'And I suppose you bought it on the proceeds of another of your paintings.'

He tapped her gently on the side of her nose. 'Mind your own business, Miss Priss.'

She would not be put off though. 'Yes, all right, it's *not* my business,' she said earnestly, 'but don't you ever think of saving your money, instead of spending it all the time?'

Nik shook his head sorrowfully. 'Spoken like a true fledgling bank manager. But life's for living—

now, my sweet—not in some indefinite future that
may never come. And if it gives me pleasure to give
you pleasure——' for a moment their eyes locked,
and she knew that he was not any longer talking
about a silver bracelet '—well, I shall. Now, let's
have a coffee, shall we?'

Catherine leaned back in her wicker chair in the
cool of the blue and white awning, gazing round
at the harbour. Through a screen of scarlet ger-
aniums and climbing plants, which served as a
divider between this café and the next, she could
glimpse the Aegean. Fishing boats bobbed on its
sparkling blue surface, while further out one of the
white-hulled ferry boats headed in from the
mainland. A mule cart trundled past from the docks
area, incongruously laden with the latest in high-
tech office equipment, and she smiled to herself.

'What's the matter?' Nik must have been
watching her as he lounged back, his fingers idly
toying with his unopened sugar sachet.

'Oh, I was just thinking.' She couldn't resist an
impish smile. 'No wonder you're so laid-back—
living here on Skiathos all the time, I mean.' When
he raised his brows enquiringly, she elaborated, 'I
don't think I'd ever want to do any work if I lived
here—certainly not sit in a bank all day.'

'Which is why you'll be counting the days till
you're back in England, no doubt,' he responded
drily. 'But what about when you're married? Will
Julian want you to *do* anything then?'

'Well, actually, Julian——' She stopped dead.

'Julian?'

His silky voice prompted her, and she went on reluctantly, 'He'd like me to give up work immediately.'

'And will you?'

'I don't think so. I don't really see myself just as a decorative wife and hostess.'

She grimaced slightly, then bit her lip. How could she be so disloyal to Julian—and with this man of all men?

A young woman was wheeling a white-padded baby buggy through the maze of tables and chairs, and beside her a toddler in a pink, lace-trimmed dress was lurching along, her chubby, dimpled knees growing further apart at every step. Just when she came alongside them she staggered, and Catherine instinctively caught her hands to steady her. The child gave them both a lovely, four-tooth smile, fluttered her long eyelashes at Nik, who responded with a wink, then tottered off.

Catherine smiled softly after her, then, meeting Nik's equivocal dark-blue gaze, felt her smile fade.

'So,' he resumed, 'Julian wants you to be wife, hostess—and mother, surely?'

'Mother? What do you mean? Oh——' She broke off in confusion. Somehow, children had never once featured in Julian's discussions of their rosy, meticulously planned future together.

'If you were *my* wife——' Nik was studying with unashamed interest the play of emotions she knew must be sweeping over her face '—motherhood would figure very high on my list. Quite a long way above decorative hostess.'

If you were my wife. To be Nik's wife...

'I——' She stared at him, her hazel eyes widening, then feeling herself colour deeply, bent forward to pick up her bag, which was propped against the table leg.

'Allow me.' Nik's hand went to it at the same instant, and between them they dropped it, scattering half the contents over the cobbles.

Before she could move, he was down on his haunches, piling back in her comb, make-up bag and travellers' cheques. Her wallet was lying open and he reached for it, then, as he went to take up a folded piece of cartridge paper which had fallen from it, Catherine suddenly jerked into life.

'No—leave it. I'll do it.'

He glanced up at her, but before she could move, dropped the wallet onto the table in front of her and opened the paper. Still looking at it, he straightened up and sank back into his chair.

'Quite a good likeness, wasn't it?' There was rather an odd expression on his face.

When she did not speak, he pushed the paper across to her and she stared down at it—although she knew every line of the sketch by heart, every detail of the way she'd been smiling, tossing back her fair hair. But he'd also caught a wistfulness in her eyes, which she'd never noticed until this instant.

She forced a light laugh. 'Good heavens—I'd forgotten I'd still got that.'

She went to crumple it in her hand but he was too swift for her. He unpeeled her fingers, smoothed out the creases, then refolded it and slipped it into his hip pocket, while Catherine fought the urge to hurl herself at him and snatch it, yelling, It's mine! Give it back to me.

'Aren't you going to throw it away?' she found herself asking coolly.

He gave her a slanted smile. 'An early work by Nik Demetrios? Just think—it may be worth a fortune one day. Someone, perhaps a hundred years from now, will buy it in a London saleroom, then start a hunt for the girl. Who was the beautiful young girl with the wistful eyes?'

She started. So he, too, had glimpsed that fleeting expression. Well, of course—he was the artist, wasn't he? And he'd probably seen much, much more than wistfulness in that young, far too revealing face...

'And somebody will come forward and say, I'm almost certain that is Catherine, my grandmother, who, once upon a time, as in all the best fairy stories, went on holiday to Greece and met a handsome young painter.'

'Don't be such a fool,' she said, but the pain in her chest was almost unbearable.

'Oh, I'm sorry.' Nik clapped a hand to his brow. 'I quite forgot—there won't be any grandchildren, will there, because children don't figure in your plans?'

Under cover of the table, her hands clenched.

'I never said that,' she said tautly, then drew a long, deep breath. 'Please, Nik—we don't have to be fighting all the time. Can't we be friends? After all, we were, years ago.' She leaned forward, her eyes pleading.

'No—we can't be *friends*.' His voice was all at once harsh, and she drew back as though he'd struck her.

'You mean, because of the house? But if we're civilised, surely we can sort it out—you know, whoever loses gives in gracefully and——'

'I *never* give in gracefully.' There was a hard implacability in his features which made her shiver suddenly. 'But in fact it is nothing to do with the house.'

'What, then? An impossible clash of personalities—is that it? You've made it clear enough that you don't like me any more.'

She gave him a small smile, but when he didn't reply she went on, her voice unsteady, 'Why didn't you come back, Nik? That day after you—I mean——'

'I know quite well what you mean,' he broke in. 'That day, after I—kissed you. But you see, *ghatahi*, I did come back.'

'The next day? But I was on the beach all the time, and——'

'I know.' His lips twisted slightly. 'I sat up on the headland watching you, walking up and down at the edge of the sea, pretending to search for shells—but all the time you were waiting for me.'

Had she been so transparent? 'So you were just playing a cruel game with me,' she burst out, all the eight-year-old pain in her voice.

'No, I was *not* playing with you. In fact, it was the hardest thing I've ever done in my life to stop myself racing down to the beach and snatching you up in my arms.'

'But——' the joy was surging through her '—why didn't you?'

'I didn't dare—because, feeling the way I did, and being, of course,' a self-mocking grimace, 'a young, hot-blooded Greek male, there was only one way things could have ended. And you were still— a child. So I stayed away.'

'I see,' she murmured. Her eyes were fixed on her empty coffee cup and she could not lift them, afraid that he would see the expression on her face.

'And now—eight years on—we cannot be *friends*, as you put it, precisely because you are no longer a child. What is between us now, Catherine, is no boy and girl relationship.'

'There's *nothing* between us,' she exclaimed loudly.

Reaching out, he took her hand, his thumb stroking across her palm. 'Oh, but there is,' he said softly. 'And you know it as well as I do.'

Mesmerised by that gently moving thumb, she could only stare at him as everything else—the buzz of conversation around them, a ship's engine in the harbour, the slap of water against a pleasure boat's hull—faded to nothing.

'We cannot be friends, Catherine—but we *shall* be lovers.'

He beckoned to the waiter, peeled off a couple of bank notes and dropped them on the plate, then, as she still sat frozen in her seat, said calmly, 'Shall we go?'

CHAPTER FIVE

NIK eased back the throttle slightly and turned off the road to pull up outside the small village mini-market. Catherine, who had been struggling to stay on by clinging to the pillion rather than twine her arms round his waist as she had done on the downward journey, clambered off.

As she followed him into the store, he announced matter-of-factly, seemingly oblivious of the tumult of emotions warring within her, 'We need to stock up with food.'

'You must let me pay my share,' she said coolly. That was the best way to treat him, she'd decided, on her precarious ride out of town—cool and distant, and maybe *that* way she would freeze him off.

'But you are my guest—on Skiathos,' he added as she opened her mouth to protest, so she clamped her lips shut, while at the same time resolving that before she left the island she'd make sure that he was not one single drachma out of pocket.

She scowled at his back at he picked up a wire basket. How was it that, even though he just sauntered indolently through life, somehow he always got his own way with her, even over something as trivial as a food bill? And if he could do

75

that, what was to stop him besting her over much bigger issues, like the house—or even——?

'What do you fancy for lunch?'

'Oh, I don't mind.' Somehow she managed a careless tone. 'An omelette would be nice.'

'OK,' he replied easily. 'I'll buy some eggs. Can you get half a dozen yogurts?' He jerked a thumb in the direction of one of the cold cabinets.

There were rows of tubs, all looking more or less identical and covered in squiggly Greek writing, and she hung over them hesitantly before picking out a couple.

'Are these right?'

'No, they're cheese. Look—it says *tiri*. Those are yogurt—*ghiaourti*.' He grinned down at her. 'I really will have to start giving you some private Greek lessons. Oh, and pass over that tin of honey—we'll have yogurt and honey for our breakfast tomorrow.'

Our breakfast tomorrow...a shared intimacy. And there was something—well, intimate in the way he said it, almost as if it was a foregone conclusion that before the night was out they would be——

'Do you fancy that?' He was looking down at her, a faint smile curving his lips, as if he had plucked that appalling thought from her mind.

'Yes, I remember the honey from last time,' she said stiffly, and turned away to the check-out...

'I'll see to these.'

Glad of the excuse to move, Catherine scooped

the lunch dishes together and retreated to the kitchen without a glance at Nik, who was sprawled in one of the recliner chairs, a cup of coffee balanced on his stomach. Sliding the plates into the sink, she flicked on the tap, staring at the little whirlpools of bubbles as the water gushed down.

She didn't know how she'd got through lunch, every forkful of that feather-light omelette turning to dry ashes in her mouth. Trapped opposite Nik, those devastating words in the café hanging in the air between them, sparking electricity like an approaching storm, she'd barely been able to speak to him. We shall be lovers ... Quite deliberately, he'd chosen to raise the stakes of this game they were playing—or rather, that he was playing—sky-high.

'I'll dry.'

Nik was at her shoulder, silent as a cat, and the plate she was holding slipped back into the water.

'There's no need.' She did not look at him. 'They'll soon dry.'

'All right,' he replied equably, but then, just when she thought he'd taken himself off again, without warning his arms slid round her waist from behind.

As she went to twist away, his hold tightened, locking her in against him, so that she was made abruptly aware of every line of his body, the soft curve of her buttocks crushed against his lean, sinewy thighs, her shoulders pinned against his broad chest.

She went rigid but then stood, her head slightly bent, not even attempting to struggle free.

'Let me go. Please, Nik.'

'You know,' he remarked conversationally, 'I was reading the other day about an interesting survey carried out in—Japan, I think it was. It appears that among the erogenous zones on a woman's body, the nape of the neck is extremely sensitive to a man's kisses. Did you read that survey, Catherine?'

'No,' she replied, stiff-lipped.

'I can't remember the exact spot—I think it was something like an inch below the hairline.' As she felt him move the tendrils of hair aside with his fingertips she shivered slightly, then his warm lips brushed across her neck. 'Is that it, do you think?'

'No, it isn't,' she said through set teeth.

'Hmmm. How about this, then?'

His mouth moved a fraction, sliding across her smooth skin and setting up an electric charge which made her whole body give a jolt then begin to vibrate softly. In the water in front of her, one hand gripped the other, until she felt the nails dig into the flesh.

'Sorry to disappoint you,' she muttered. 'That survey must have got it wrong.' But she had to bite hard on the inner part of her mouth to subdue the sensations that were all but overwhelming her.

Against her skin, she felt Nik smile—a wolf's smile.

'Little liar,' he whispered, then opening his mouth he took a ridge of soft flesh between his teeth and began gently flicking the very top of his tongue to and fro across it.

The seductive mix of slight pain from his teeth and intense pleasure from that tongue-point was all but unbearable. Catherine felt a tide of raw sensation, vivid and intense, swirl through her body until it became heavy and lethargic, and the blood coagulated, to run slow and thick through her veins.

She gasped, and a violent shudder shook her from head to foot, then, just before that terrifying leaden languor could take her and destroy her completely, she tore free of his grasp and swung round on him. There was a faint line of colour etched along his cheekbones, a muscle flicking tautly beside his mouth.

'I've told you——' her voice cracked, but she went on '—leave me alone, damn you.'

'But, *koukla*, are you quite sure that is what you want?'

'Yes, I am—quite sure.' Looking down at her hands she saw, first the line of nail marks across the back of her left hand, one oozing a tiny pinprick of blood, and then her ring. 'Perhaps you've forgotten, but I'm engaged.'

'No, I hadn't forgotten. Had you?' His tone was almost pleasant, but his eyes were steel-hard. 'Come through to your bedroom when you've finished here.'

As her head jerked up, he went on smoothly, 'I promised to move my paintings out of your way, remember. You can give me a hand.'

Out of the corner of her eye, she watched him lope off with that panther-like tread of his. He was even whistling softly under his breath—so sure of himself, so arrogant. Damn him! She shot a last killing glance at his back as it disappeared, then banged her clenched fists down hard on the rim of the sink.

What had she told herself? Freeze him off. And now, the very first time he came near her, she'd done everything but melt in his arms. Was it Greece, or was it him, that was making her act so—so out of character? she asked herself despairingly. Whatever it was, if she was going to fight him she had to keep on equal ground, not be on the point of surrendering to him every single waking moment.

But wasn't that exactly what the devious swine intended? she thought with a sudden flash of insight. That threat, promise—whatever it was—back by the harbour, and now this consummately skilled mini seduction; weren't they both just clever ploys in the same master plan, aimed at sending her back to England, screaming for protection from Julian and leaving him in sole possession here? Yes, of course they were. What an underhand devil he was. Well, she wasn't going to scuttle off like a timid little mouse—no way.

'At last.' As she appeared in the bedroom doorway, Nik came towards her with an armful of paintings. 'Take these to my studio at the far end.'

'Oh, certainly, sir. Anything you say, sir.'

Snatching them off him, she carried them along to the room he had indicated, dumping them against the wall beside a pile of others. She was about to return for the next load when she paused and looked around her, fascinated in spite of herself to see Nik's studio. There was an easel, several palettes and a paint-stained smock which had fallen from its peg. She picked it up and held it in her arms, catching the faint elusive scent that was Nik Demetrios and no other man. She stood motionless for a moment, then angrily rehung it and went back to her room.

'Right, that's the lot.' He gave her another armful then followed her, carrying one large canvas—a half-finished view from the veranda of the villa.

She set her load down as Nik, his back to her, went down on his haunches, carefully setting the canvas upright. He had changed—of course—back into his shorts, and his back was bare—a smooth expanse of highly strokeable brown satin. Catherine hastily lowered her eyes, and instead found herself staring fixedly at his neat, firm buttocks, strained tautly against the faded denim.

He turned his head sharply, as though sensing her gaze on his body, and their eyes met. For a few seconds, the air seemed to become stiflingly hot, the heat almost burning her, then she roused herself and said jerkily, 'You have a lot of paintings here.'

Getting slowly to his feet, he came over to her. 'This room is north-facing and it has this huge window.' He gestured towards the wide shutters, through which the clear, intense light poured. 'Gerald let me turn it into a studio to use whenever I wanted.'

'I didn't realise you knew him that well.'

In fact, she'd really known nothing of Nik that last time—not even his surname or where he lived. He'd just appeared each day, and she'd accepted that. And she'd never told her grandfather about him—just hugged the secret of their meetings to herself...

He shrugged slightly. 'I didn't—not when you were here before. He was my father's friend then. I got to know him later.'

'I see.' He was so close to her that she felt her skin begin to tingle, as though he was actually touching it, and she inched imperceptibly away. 'Can I look at your paintings?'

'Of course.'

As she turned to them he went and leaned against the window frame, his head against his crooked arm, watching her. They were seascapes mainly—sweeping, vivid, brimming with the restless movement of the sea as it broke on rocks or flung itself down on to the sand.

But then she stooped down by another stack against the far wall, realising as she turned them over, one by one, that they were all of the same subject—a woman, young and very beautiful.

Sometimes her long black hair was left hanging loose on her shoulders, sometimes it was coiled into a heavy knot, but it was always the same face.

Conscious of Nik's gaze, she flicked through half a dozen more then stopped dead as she pulled back a full-length nude study. The girl was sprawled on a bed in a tangle of sheets, one hand cradled behind her head, staring out at the viewer. Her clothes still lay on a corner of the bed—Catherine could make out a flowered skirt and the ruffles of a white blouse. It was not the clothes which arrested her gaze and held it, though, but the dark eyes of the girl—drowsy, and full of a languorous sensuality.

She was—yes, voluptuous, that was the word. Her pale, creamy skin was so alive that Catherine could almost feel it, her rounded limbs relaxed into the mattress in the aftermath of lovemaking.

'Do you like it?' Nik's voice seemed to come from a very long way away, through a greenish haze.

'It's very well done,' she replied woodenly.

'That's Elena—my favourite model.' Was it her imagination, or had Nik's tone warmed slightly, as if with remembered, shared rapture? 'She has often—sat for me.'

I'll bet she has, Catherine thought savagely.

'What's the matter, my sweet?' he asked softly. 'Not jealous, surely?'

'*Jealous*?' She gave a scornful laugh. 'Of a girl who's obviously no better than she ought to be?'

'What a very—prim phrase to describe something so beautiful.' Nik's caustic voice taunted her,

and she knew that he was not referring to the girl
herself.

Letting the painting fall back, she got awkwardly
to her feet and winced slightly as pins and needles
shot through one foot. As she lurched forward, he
caught hold of her, pulling her into his arms. At
once his mouth was against hers, but she forced
herself to stand unresponsive, thinking—with the
small part of her brain which was still capable of
thought—remember, it's just a ploy. She *wouldn't*
respond.

But as she tasted the sweetness of him, felt the
surge of power as he pressed her to him, her own
treacherous body betrayed her, bypassing her
fuddled brain. Her fingers went to his shoulders,
gripping them convulsively, and her mouth opened
wider under his, as if inviting his deeper thrust.

He released her at last though but still held her
by the elbows and she stared up at him, too dazed
at first to focus on him clearly. Then she saw the
faint smile playing round his lips and could have
fallen on the floor, beating her fists in self-fury.

'You're w-wasting your time, Nik. If you think
you're going to seduce me out of my rights, I
promise you—you won't.'

'Brave words.' He regarded her thoughtfully for
a moment. 'Are you a betting woman, *koukla*?'

'No, I'm not.'

'Just as well.' A slanting smile. 'Would you like
me to paint you, Catherine?'

'What?' She gazed at him, barely hearing the question under the tumult of her racing heartbeat. 'You mean like this, I suppose?' Her eyes slid unwillingly to the painting.

'Certainly, if you like——'

'I do *not* like——'

'No, I didn't think you would.' The contempt made her raw nerves smart. 'But I assure you——' he put a hand to his heart—if he had one '—when I paint a nude, my whole mind is on light and shade, skin texture, and nothing else.'

'You mean like with Elena?' The words came out before she could keep them back. 'She was just light and shade, I suppose.'

'Well, perhaps not quite.' And Catherine could have flung herself at him to scratch off that fleeting smile, where she glimpsed the same sleepy sensuality as in the painting. 'But I'll do a nice, highly respectable portrait for you.'

'Well——' She regarded him, lips pursed. The thought of spending hours in Nik's close company was appalling. On the other hand, though, while he was painting her, at least he wouldn't be sneaking off to the lawyer...

'You could give it to Julian as a wedding present,' he said cajolingly. 'If I do it well enough, of course.'

'Well,' she repeated slowly, 'I was going to give him one of those new CD players—he's very fond of classical music. And what's wrong with that?' as Nik wrinkled his nose.

'Nothing. It's just that I'm a jazz fan myself, especially blues.'

Yes, you would be, she thought. All that throbbing, insistent beat that makes you want to lose your self-control and lie naked in a man's arms——

'Of course, if Julian would prefer a nude...'

She went rigid in every muscle. He really was a mind-reader—he had to be. 'I've told you—no.'

'Ah, well—a head and shoulders will be enough of a challenge.'

'I haven't said yet that I'm going to pose for you,' she said coldly. 'But *if* I do, why is it such a challenge?'

'To reveal the real Catherine, of course.'

'What do you mean?' She gave him an uneasy look.

'To strip away the mask, to show the tantalising things that are hidden behind that pretty face, those cool hazel eyes.'

'But there's nothing hidden. This *is* the real me,' she protested, but he only gave her another of those crooked little smiles.

'I'll choose what you're to wear.'

'It's *my* portrait—I'll choose,' she snarled at his back, then hurried along behind him to her room.

'This will do.' Nik dropped the other outfits he had removed from her wardrobe on to the bed, and tossed at her a long-sleeved, draw-string neck blouse in white Indian cotton, together with a dark, Provençal-patterned skirt. 'Get changed.'

'But I don't really like that blouse. I only brought it because it's cool.'

'I'll sort out my gear,' was the only response, and Catherine was left scowling at the door.

She stamped her foot in frustration. What on earth had she got herself into? She must be mad. But if Julian liked it, at least it would be an original wedding gift. Would she, though, want a part of Nik for ever on their sitting-room wall?

When she went outside, he was pacing up and down the veranda. As she appeared, he muttered something in Greek, then, 'Where the hell have you been? I didn't ask you to give yourself a three-hour beauty treatment. The light's perfect at the moment.'

'Sorry.' Catherine contented herself with a hostile look from under her lashes.

'Come on.' And snatching up his easel, he swung a small canvas bag over one shoulder.

She stood on the top step. 'But aren't we going to your studio?'

'What for? I'm painting you down in the olive grove, of course.'

But she didn't want Nik to paint her there. She wanted to be painted—if at all—in the safe, *secure* confines of the studio.

'No,' she said, but he was already out of sight . . .

'Pick a bunch of flowers.' He was setting up his palette when she appeared. 'Well—what are you waiting for?' His voice was jagged with irritability, and she hastened to obey.

'Is this enough?' She held up the flowers—yellow and white daisies, bright red poppies with sooty centres, pale blue borage, lavender-pink mallows, and convolvulus like purple satin.

'Fine.' He hardly glanced at them. 'Now—sit there, against the trunk of that tree. No—not that one.' Another mutter in Greek—no doubt roughly translated as, Heaven preserve me from half-witted models—then she was pushed, fairly gently, down against the rough, gnarled bark of an olive tree. He squatted in front of her, his face screwed up in concentration.

'Put your hand against the trunk—yes, that's it. One arm lying relaxed——' relaxed? How could he possibly think she could relax a millimetre? '—on the ground, the other holding the flowers across your lap—like this.' He suddenly frowned at her. 'What have you combed your hair for?'

'I wanted it tidy, of course.'

'Tidy!' He rolled his eyes heavenwards. 'Keep still.' And his hands were tangling painfully in her hair, drawing dishevelled strands forward around her face. 'That's better.'

'But I don't——'

'Shut up. Now——' He loosened the tie of her blouse a little, easing the neckline apart so that more of her shoulders and the swell of her breasts was revealed, then, his face abstract, he arranged the folds of her skirt.

He was right. She really had become just light and shade and texture to him. She could have posed naked—and she'd have looked as good as any Elena. Aghast, she pulled herself up. What was she thinking of? Julian would be horrified if she presented him with a nude portrait, and besides ...

'I thought you were just doing a head and shoulders,' she said, as he hunkered back, studying her appraisingly.

'So did I. But that would be a waste.'

'Of what?' she demanded suspiciously.

'Of such a beautiful body, of course. Right—look at me.' Reluctantly, she raised her eyes to meet his intent blue-black gaze. 'Now, go into yourself. Think of anything you want to.'

And the image slid into her mind of herself, lying naked among the flowers, their soft petals stroking against her smooth skin as a man bent towards her ...

'Yes, that's it.' Dimly she heard Nik's voice.

The man's face was in shadow, but somehow she knew it wasn't Julian. Oh, Julian—where are you? she cried out silently. But then Nik got up, went back to his easel and picked up a brush ...

A little breeze came flicking through the grove, rustling the olive leaves and cooling her clammy brow where damp wisps of hair clung. Unobtrusively, she flexed her legs and felt the muscles, cramped by hours of stillness, protest, then she stole a glance at Nik.

He was totally absorbed, as he had been all afternoon, a little frown of concentration between his brows. Seen from here, the sunlight and shadow playing over his face, he looked younger—eight years younger. As she looked at him, her eyes heavy-lidded with memory, a lock of black hair tumbled forward over his brow as he bent down to reach something out of his bag.

She longed to reach forward and smooth back that dark lock, stroke away those frown lines, and as her gaze travelled slowly down over his face to his bare, muscular shoulders, she felt strange sensations stir in her, until every part of her body seemed to grow inert and yielding.

Sudden panic flared in her. What on earth was she doing? After his terrifying words at that harbour café, such erotic fantasies were the very last thing she should be indulging in. She moved involuntarily, and Nik snapped, 'For heaven's sake, keep still.'

In a desperate attempt to force her mind to safer ground, she said, 'What painters do you like? Apart from yourself, of course.'

He grimaced. 'I don't like myself most of the time. Just occasionally, I'm half-way satisfied with something I produce. Why? Who do you like?'

'Well, I don't know much about painting, but I do love Van Gogh. All those swirls and dazzling colours. I've got a print of one with a skylark hovering above the cornfield—you can almost feel the wind rustling the corn, and hear the lark singing its heart out. It cheers me up on bad days.'

She smiled at him, but he did not return the smile.

'But surely, *agape mou*,' he said softly, 'engaged to the youngest bank manager ever, and with a perfect future all meticulously planned, you don't have any bad days.'

He was like a cat, pouncing as soon as the mouse made the slightest false move. 'Doesn't everybody?' she replied tersely.

'Perhaps. But you know, Catherine, you really have grown into a woman of contradictions.'

What was he getting at now? 'How do you mean?' she asked warily.

'That ice-maiden act of yours——'

'It is *not* an act! And anyway——'

'Yet you fell for that desert painting of mine, and now you tell me that you find Van Gogh irresistible. A strange, potent cocktail—half frozen ice, half sensual fire.'

'What nonsense!' She forced a careless laugh. 'Just because I happen to like a lovely painting.' And deliberately turning her head away, she stared into the distance...

'That's it.' Nik flung down his brush and stretched luxuriously, then, taking her by the hand, he pulled her upright. 'All right?'

He himself looked drained, lines of fatigue on his face.

'I think so.' Cautiously, she eased her aching back and shoulders, realising as she did so that long shadows were slanting across the grove, while the low sun outlined Nik's silhouette, gilding the ends of his hair. 'Are you always so hard on your sitters?' she asked, a few drops of acid still in her tone.

'Not always.' His voice was a soft purr. Was he thinking of Elena, lying on that bed, and what they had done together among those rumpled sheets? Oh, damn Elena—and damn Nik, she thought suddenly and strode off towards the house, leaving him to pack up his gear.

She was in the kitchen, putting her flowers in a jug of water, when he arrived.

'You needn't bother with them,' he said. 'You'll need fresh ones tomorrow.'

'Tomorrow? You haven't finished it, then?'

'Of course not. I've only just done the groundwork so far.'

So there were going to be more sessions down in the olive grove, more hours when her thoughts would be free to roam untrammelled...

'Can I see what you've done so far?'

'No—not till it's finished. And only then if I'm happy with it.' And he headed off towards his studio.

'Shall I start getting the meal?'

He turned back to her. 'No, don't bother. I fancy eating down at the taverna.'

'Oh, so it's open tonight, then?' That waspish note was back in her voice—a note she never used with anyone except this infuriating man.

'Could be,' he replied laconically. 'I'll go and shower—and shave.' He ran his fingers over his dark stubble and grinned provokingly. 'I certainly need one, don't you think? Or maybe you prefer me like this?'

'It makes not the slightest difference to me,' she said woodenly, and, with another slanting grin, he went off.

She waited in her room until she heard the bathroom door open and his bedroom door close. When she went in, there were the imprints of damp feet, the arches well-defined, the toes spread. The subtle tang of aftershave hung in the air, and she stood for a moment before suddenly flinging open the shutters, then walked over to the shower, carefully avoiding those firm, purposeful footprints.

When she went out on to the veranda he had changed into a long-sleeved white shirt and tight, hip-hugging pale grey trousers, and was sitting on the top step, chin on his hand, gazing into space. She halted in the doorway, unwilling to disturb him, shy even, but he must have heard her for, glancing round, he got to his feet. He stood looking at her, not speaking—and all at once she began to be very sorry that she had opted for this dress out of all the others that she could have chosen tonight.

He surveyed her from top to toe, very slowly, as though to take in every detail of her. Then he lifted his gaze to her face again, and as their eyes met and held, something bright and dangerous seemed to flare in the breathless air between them, blaze up, then fall back to earth once more with the faintest hiss.

'Is—is it too dressy—for the taverna, I mean?' She put a nervous hand up to her hair, smoothing down the shiny bob which lay on her shoulders.

'No.' But he spoke absently, as if he barely heard her.

'Because I can change if it is.' Really, the pale blue crêpe shirt-waister she'd hesitated over would have been far more suitable—and much wiser than a straight, above-the-knee sliver of pink silk, sleeveless and with a low-cut scoop neckline.

'No, don't change.' He roused himself and gave her a sidelong look. 'And what does Julian think of that dress?'

'Well——' she hesitated, then her innate honesty made her pull a rueful face. 'Actually, he hasn't seen it.'

'So, you're wearing it just for me. I'm flattered.'

'No, of course I'm not,' she retorted hotly. 'It's simply that it was an impulse buy, just before I came out here. I saw this, and fell for it.'

'An impulse buy? But I didn't think an aspiring bank manager was allowed to be impulsive—or a sensualist. Pink silk, against a woman's skin, softer than a lover's caress or——'

'Shall we go?' Catherine cut in loudly. 'I'm hungry.'

The small taverna, set back from the road among olive trees, was festooned with strings of fairy lights. It was crowded—and very noisy—and for a second Catherine wished that they'd stayed back at the villa. But that would have meant another intimate meal for two so it was far better to be down here, in the anonymous security of this boisterous throng. As soon as they appeared, though, a group of young men over by the bar called to Nik.

'I won't be a moment. Sit down there.' He pointed to a small table, then made his way across to them.

A young girl brought a menu, and under cover of studying it Catherine looked over the top, her eyes following Nik as he instantly became the ebullient centre of a laughing, back-slapping throng.

It must be marvellous to be like that, she thought wistfully. So much better than the way she'd been brought up. Had her parents ever had any real enjoyment in life—and did Julian? Of course they did, all three of them, she told herself angrily. How could she be so disloyal? It was just that they took their pleasures in a different, more undemonstrative kind of way. Nik was an extrovert, brimming with uninhibited, animal vitality. And that was all right now that he was still the right side of thirty, but was he going to go on all his life in this happy-go-lucky, irresponsible way?

Really, he was so like her grandfather—that 'aged hippy', as she'd once heard her father refer to him. And of course, it was here, wasn't it, in this very taverna, that Gramps had got himself involved in that ridiculous wager, which had led to all the trouble she was in now. No, her parents—and

Julian—had a depth, a solidity, which Nik could never possess . . .

'Sorry about that.' He slid into the chair opposite her. 'But I've known Giorgios—the one in the Harvard University sweatshirt—since he was so high, and it's his—what do you say?—stag night. He's getting married tomorrow.'

'You go and join them,' she said, seizing on the chance. 'Honestly, I don't mind at——'

'Sssh.' Leaning across he put up a finger and brushed it across her lips in a mirror-image of that gentle caress of a kiss down on the beach. 'Now, what do you want to eat?'

'What?' She stared at him blindly, the touch of his skin still lingering unnervingly against hers, then snatched up the menu. 'I'd like Greek salad to start, then moussaka, please,' she said, with a feeble attempt at her usual incisiveness.

And when the waitress appeared, she took a bread roll from the small wicker basket and began to butter it . . .

They were sipping the aromatic Greek coffee and brandy, when she realised that the open-air area in the centre of the taverna was being cleared. A small group of musicians took their places, striking up a few preliminary chords, and straight away half a dozen stag party lads leapt to their feet, to much ironic applause and cat-calls. They formed a row, hands resting lightly on each other's shoulders, then one of them spotted Nik and beckoned urgently to him. With a wry little shrug at her he stood up and went across to join them.

Catherine sat back, glancing round the taverna and saw a group of young English women at a nearby table. They were watching the men—no, they weren't, she realised with a sudden jolt—they were watching Nik. Their eyes were trained on him, devouring him, greedily, avidly, and her lip curled slightly. It's demeaning, she thought, no woman should ever look at a man like that. And then the music began.

It was slow and soft at first, and the men began to dance to and fro in a sinuous movement, like a snake coiling on itself. As the harsh, slightly metallic music became louder, more insistent, the rhythm of their bodies, coupled with the strange, almost eastern beat, began weaving a spell in her brain until all she was conscious of was the shifting pattern made by Nik's white shirt, his face, frowning in concentration as he traced the intricate, convoluted steps, and his dark head, that tantalising lock of hair flopping forward again.

The dance was intensely, blatantly sexual, the slow beginning, the inexorable build-up, the men's bodies—or rather Nik's body, for she was aware now only of him—swaying, legs stamping, hips and pelvis thrusting forward, and finally the climax, swift and shattering.

And it was then that Catherine, her hands sweating as she clutched them together in her lap, her whole body throbbing from the blood which pulsed through her veins, realised that she was staring at Nik with naked, undeniable greed and avidity.

CHAPTER SIX

HAD she gone completely off her head? She bit her lip but a small moan of misery escaped her. Those erotic fantasies in the olive grove this afternoon, and now this. Within a single day of setting foot in Greece again, she, a cool, self-contained twenty-four-year-old, was behaving like an immature teenager in the grip of her first crush. Was that it? Was she—seduced once more by the sheer insidious *Greekness* of it all—reliving those adolescent torments of eight years ago? And for the same man? Whatever it was, she had to put a rein on those runaway emotions—and fast!

Dimly she became aware that the music had changed and the line of dancers was breaking up. Two of the stag party moved in smoothly on the table where the English girls were sitting, while Nik stood talking to the happy bridegroom-to-be. As she stared at him, dry-mouthed, he turned as though aware of her eyes on him and looked directly across at her. Then he clapped the other man on the back and began winding his way back through the crowded tables.

He stood over her, that lazy smile which she was beginning to know so well curving the corners of his mouth, and held out his hands. 'Come and dance.'

It was more a command than a polite invitation, but she shrank back into her chair. Dance with Nik, have that beautiful, oh, so male body pressed close to hers, hip against hip, thigh against thigh?

'Thanks, but I'd really rather not.'

But he was already lifting her effortlessly out of her chair and into his arms, and steering her out on to the dance floor, one hand in the small of her back. Fleetingly she caught envious glances from the English girls, but they did nothing at all to ease her supercharged nerves.

She held herself rigidly at first, determined not to succumb one iota to the power of Nik's body. For that was all it was, this maelstrom of emotions—body chemistry. Take one vibrant, virile body, she told herself scornfully, allow its potent masculinity to be exerted over one female body, shake the hormones well, and place the two in close proximity on a crowded dance floor, with a midnight-blue velvet sky overhead...

But gradually, inexorably with every skilful twirl, Nik was drawing her closer to him, moulding her to him. She knew it, and yet she was utterly helpless to resist, even when he drew her against his chest, his arm curving round her shoulders, his cheek on her hair. His thumb softly stroked across the top of her collarbone, then his hand eased under the neck of her dress to lie across her shoulder, the pulse at his wrist beating against her bare flesh.

The gesture was half tender, half erotic, and it woke those strange, swirling sensations in her again, so that when the music died away she could only stand for a moment, staring up at him, her eyes slumbrous, her lips parted tremulously.

Only for a moment, though. As the talk and laughter flowed around them, she roused herself as though from a deep sleep and jerked back out of his arms.

'I—I'm leaving now—I'm very tired. But please, you stay.'

She plunged headlong off the floor and almost ran down the lane from the taverna, stumbling in the dried wheel ruts. But as she turned up the track to the villa, above the rasping of her own breathing she heard Nik, calling her peremptorily to stop. Reluctantly, she slowed and seconds later he came up to her.

'You forgot this.' He held out her small clutch bag and she took it, not looking at him.

'Thank you,' she said tautly, 'but you shouldn't have bothered. You could have given it to me in the morning.'

'I was ready to leave. Come on.'

He rested an arm lightly round her shoulders and she stiffened, but then let him lead her on up the track. In the warm night air all her senses were sharpened, heightening not only the already intoxicating fragrance of the honeysuckle hedge which ran to their left, but also that individual scent, the subtle mix of aftershave, sandalwood soap and maleness that was Nik, and which was invading every pore in her body. She could feel it weaving strange patterns in the computer of her brain, programming those instinctive chemical reactions within her once again.

Then, when they were almost at the house, an invisible bird began to sing, its song so intensely sweet that Catherine caught her breath at the perfect beauty.

'What is it?' she whispered.

'A nightingale,' Nik breathed in her ear. 'I think he's in that old poplar tree over there.'

He pulled her gently into the deep shade of an olive tree and they stood motionless as the liquid song cascaded and bubbled in the air around them. At last though, down in the village a dog barked fiercely, there was a rustle of leaves, then silence.

'It was so beautiful.' Catherine, still under the spell of that pure perfection of sound, gave a faint, tremulous sigh.

'There are a lot of nightingales on the island. Didn't you ever hear them last time?'

'Perhaps. I can't remember.' But never so lovely, so heart-wrenching as tonight, standing here in the shelter of Nik's arm.

As she went to turn away, his grip tightened, turning her round to him. Above her in the glimmering darkness his face was a blur, and his breath was against her mouth, sweet with the wine he had drunk.

'Catherine.' Even his voice added to the bewitching spell of the night, warm, husky, with a sensual throb in it, and when he ran his fingers across her lips, she quivered violently.

'No—no, Nik—*please*!' The broken sentence ended on a little pleading cry, and she struggled to break free. 'Please—let me go.'

She gazed up at him, a tear glistening on her cheek, and he caught it on his thumb, flicking it away.

'Catherine,' he repeated, 'you can break away from me tonight. I will allow you to do that——' and he opened his hand, releasing her wrist '—but we both know, you and I, that it is only a matter of time before you no longer fight against what is inevitable between us.'

'No!'

'*Yes*, my sweet. It was there eight years ago, when you were still a child—and now that you are a woman, as surely as the sun will rise over that hilltop tomorrow, very soon you will lie unresisting in my arms, welcoming me, wanting me just as I want you.'

He stood there, making no attempt to touch her, yet deep inside him she sensed a dark force, pitting the strength of his will against hers. She felt it swirl against her, knocking her off balance, so that she was drowning, helpless to save herself.

But she *wasn't* helpless—she would *not* surrender. Drawing on every last fibre of strength, she stepped back from him, putting up her hands as though to rupture that dark force-field.

'No. I tell you—no,' she hurled defiantly in his face. 'I don't want you—I never have, and I never shall!' Then, stumbling past him, she ran off up the track.

She was in her bedroom when she finally heard him arrive back. As she stood motionless, her eyes wide, staring at the door, there were footsteps. A door opened and closed, then another, and then there was silence. She released a long, shuddering sob of breath, then reached for her nightie and, automaton-like, began to undress.

An endless time later, she was still gazing at the narrow band of moonlight which filtered through the crack in her shutters. Peering at her small bedside clock, she saw it click round to one-twenty, and suppressed a groan. Unable to bear the thin sheet against her sweating body a moment longer, she flung it back and sat up. She had to get some air or she'd suffocate.

Reaching for her pink gingham housecoat, she slipped it on, then soundlessly opened her door and crept out into the passage. All was silent— somebody, at least, was flat out, sleeping the sleep of the just. Outside on the veranda she caught up her espadrilles, which were lying where she had kicked them off earlier, and tiptoed away.

Just as she reached the beach, the moon emerged from a little cloud, tipping the ebony waves with silver. Wrapping her arms across her chest, she walked slowly across the sand, wriggled her feet out of her espadrilles, then stood at the very edge of the sea, so that the next wavelet just caught her toes. The water was cool and inviting, and she knew exactly what it would be like—dark, opaque silk against her bare skin.

One night that other summer, unable to sleep—and racked then, too, with thoughts of this same man—she'd come down here and, on a sudden crazy impulse, dragged off her clothes and swum naked. She pulled a rueful face. Sometimes, she thought it was the only impulsive thing she'd ever done in her life. Sometimes even, she wondered if she'd dreamed it, that solitary moonlit swim...

Back home, her mother, returning early one afternoon from a shopping trip, had found her sunbathing topless in their secluded back garden, and been scandalised. 'Darling, whatever would Mr Jenkins say?'

The young Catherine had wanted to reply that their seventy-year-old neighbour would probably hobble off in search of his binoculars, but then, shooting a glance at her mother's horrified face, she'd thought better of it and instead reached for her bikini top.

Her mother had sighed and shaken her head. 'That Greek holiday's done you no good at all— you've done nothing but moon around since you came back. We should never have allowed you to go out there.'

They hadn't made the same mistake the next summer, of course, and then she'd left school, gone into the bank—and met Julian ...

Catherine stared down at the water, rippling around her feet, then all at once, almost in defiance—though she didn't know of what—she tore off her housecoat and nightie, dropped them on the sand and, not giving herself time to think, waded in. Taking a deep breath, she launched herself and began swimming fiercely up and down, as if to exorcise some demon from her fevered mind, then turned onto her back, revelling in the feel of the water, cool but delicious against her flesh.

Above her were the million diamond-points of the Aegean stars. Her grandfather had told her that these were the same stars beneath which Paris, Prince of Troy, had fallen besottedly in love with Helen, and ruined his whole kingdom for her sake. Gramps was probably right—you *could* do crazy things under stars like these, lose every last atom of common sense.

Abruptly, she turned on to her front and started swimming back to shore, but then she stilled, her breath frozen in her throat. A dark figure had just emerged from among the pine trees and was walking down the beach.

As she trod water silently, Nik tossed down the towel which was slung over his shoulder, then put his hands to the belt of his dark-coloured robe and shrugged it off. Catherine drew in her breath with a sudden rasping sound as she realised that he was naked. In the moonlight, she could see him clearly—a silver statue, sheer and perfect maleness.

He stood for a few seconds, gazing at the water lapping his ankles, then began wading out. He had not seen her; she was out of his line of vision, her bobbing head and shoulders hidden against the dark outline of the promontory. If she stayed perfectly still he would swim out past her and then she could make her escape.

Next moment though, something—a fish?—brushed past her legs and she gave an involuntary gasp. It was smothered almost as it left her lips, but it was enough.

'Catherine—is that you?'

'Y-yes. No—go away,' she began in panic, but he was already scything through the water towards her, his strokes so rapid that she did not even try to outswim him to shore. Instead, she forced herself to carry on treading water, until a final stroke brought him gliding smoothly alongside her, his hair sleek in the moonlight, his eyes gleaming.

'What the hell are you doing out here alone?' he demanded roughly.

'I—couldn't sleep.'

'Well, next time you're suffering from insomnia, take a walk instead.'

'I'll do just what I please.' At least, her indignation was masking something of her inner terror.

'Not while you're under my roof, you won't.'

'I am *not* under your roof,' she retorted furiously. 'And anyway, what are *you* doing, following me like this?'

'I didn't know you were here, sweetheart, or I wouldn't have bothered. When I'm starting a painting, I feel the need to unwind—alone.'

'Well, be my guest, then. I'll happily leave you in peace.' And turning her back on him, she began swimming rapidly in the direction of Turkey.

She had only managed half a dozen flurried strokes though, before a pair of strong hands seized her round the waist from behind, dragging her to an abrupt halt. She went under and resurfaced coughing and spluttering.

'Leave me——'

'Shut up. If you won't go in yourself, I'll take you in.'

As she struggled frantically to free herself, he seized her by the wrist in an iron-hard grip, swung her round, and began towing her back towards the shore.

They were in the shallows. Just a few more powerful strokes and he'd realise that——

'No! Let me go.'

She flailed a despairing kick at him, and in response he jerked her hard up against his body. Next moment, there was the shock of contact as bare flesh met bare flesh. She heard him expel his breath in a hiss as he stared at her, his eyes dark, then his arms went round her, straining her body to his so that she felt the muscle-tautening passion flare into life in him.

'No, Nik—please.'

'Yes, my sweet.'

'*No.*'

Desperately, she tried to turn her head away, but his fingers caught in her wet hair, forcing her face towards him. His lips, as they came down on hers, were cold and had the tang of salt, yet at the same time they were intensely sweet.

'My lovely Catherine,' he said against her mouth. 'I've waited so long for you, so very long, to taste your bewitching body.'

His voice was rich and thick, like Greek honey, and it acted on her like a drug so that her blood was heavy in her veins. A violent shudder shook her entire frame, and, catching her up in his arms, he carried her through the shallows, the tiny waves splashing round them.

At the sand's edge he set her down again, slowly, so that she trickled between his hands like water, the friction of their wet, slippery bodies one against the other sparking off little molten fires in her breasts, her limbs, her loins, until she had to bite on the soft inside of her mouth to stifle a moan at those unbearable, exquisite sensations.

Reaching blindly for each other, they sank to their knees on the wet sand. Nik ran his fingers down the line of her throat, then cupped one of her breasts, his hand dark against the creamy, pale mound. Lowering his head, he took the nipple between his teeth, taking it then releasing it, then taking it again, his tongue flicking round it until it engorged, straining towards his greedy mouth, as if only that could assuage its own need.

But the hunger was growing within her, not lessening, her whole body trembling and on fire with feelings that she hadn't known existed. It was as if inside her there had been a heap of tinder-dry kindling, and Nik's mouth and hands had acted like a flaring torch, so that now her entire body was in flames and burning too.

His mouth slid across to the other breast, teasing, tormenting it until she thought she would die. His hands moved down to mould her buttocks, clamping them to him so that she felt the raw, potent force of his body, and with an incoherent little sound she brought her own hands up, tangling in his hair, holding him against her breast as he suckled her.

Her eyes were open wide and staring, her head turning from side to side as the moon and stars reeled in a dizzy samba over her head—and twinkled on the tiny star-point of light on her left hand.

Julian! What was she doing, betraying him like this? The shame and humiliation slammed into her like a blow to the solar plexus, and she went rigid.

'No—no, Nik! *Please*—I don't want——'

Something of the terrified anguish in her voice must have got through to him, for he lifted his head and looked at her, his eyes blank, like a stranger's.

'I'm s-sorry.' She pressed the back of her hand to her mouth. 'But—I can't.' A convulsive shudder shook her slender frame, another and then another. 'Julian——' Her voice finally shattered into a loud sob, and putting her hands to her face she began to cry.

With an incoherent exclamation, Nik pulled her into his arms. At first she resisted, pushing desperately against him as they half knelt, half lay on the sand, but at last, unable to break his grip, she let go and he cradled her to him, stroking her hair and making little soothing sounds, until the sobs died to a long, miserable hiccup.

He held her away from him, gazing down into her wet, tear-blotched face. 'All right?' His own breathing was ragged.

'Mmm.' She tried to smile, but failed totally.

'Oh, don't look like that, *koukla*.'

His fingers dug painfully into her upper arms, but she managed not to flinch away from him.

'I'm sorry,' she whispered again. 'It was my fault.'

'It was no one's fault.' His voice was harsh. 'Least of all yours.'

He went to draw her into his arms once more, but then thrust her away from him.

'I think maybe that wouldn't be very wise,' he said wryly, and she sensed some of the tension in him ease. 'Wait a moment.'

Jack-knifing to his feet, he went across to his wrap and slipped it on. When he came back, he was carrying her nightie and housecoat and the towel.

'Up you get.'

Raising her to her feet, he rubbed her quickly with the towel and dropped the nightdress over her head. Then he slipped her arms into the sleeves of the housecoat and stood watching as she tried to do up the little buttons. But her hands were still trembling too much from the aftermath of the storm which had shaken her, and finally he put them aside and fastened every button up to her chin.

'There—that's better.' Another wry smile, which still she could not respond to.

Her hair lay on her shoulders in wet strands, and he murmured, 'You look like a mermaid—a forlorn little mermaid who doesn't quite know what's happening to her.' And, gathering up the strands into a bunch, he turbanned the towel around her head.

As she gazed up at him mutely, his mouth twisted. 'Don't worry, *koukla*—I shan't pounce on you again. Tonight is not our night.'

No, not tonight. But there would be other nights—warm Greek nights of magic, slyly treacherous, seducing her into acting in this wholly alien way...

'Oh, Catherine——' he shook his head ruefully '—why ever did you come down here tonight?'

'I told you—I couldn't sleep.' Her voice was brittle. 'I—I expect it was that coffee at the taverna. It's much stronger than I'm used to.'

'Of course.' He nodded, as though accepting her lie.

'Look,' she went on quickly, 'you stay here and have your swim. I can make my own way back—really, I can.'

He hesitated, and for an agonising moment she thought he was going to refuse, but then he gave a faint shrug. 'If you like.'

When she reached the fringe of pine trees she stopped and looked over her shoulder. Nik, his back to her, was just taking off his robe. Just for a moment she stood motionless, then turned and walked quickly away through the trees.

CHAPTER SEVEN

'COME on—out you get.'

As the shutters crashed back, flooding the room with sunlight, Catherine was instantly catapulted from a dream in which she had been trying to escape from a maze, only to find time after time every exit in the tall hedges blocked by a man's dark outline, so that each time, with a little sob of terror, she had turned and blundered away down yet another blind alley.

She opened her eyes, then, as she saw Nik standing at the foot of the bed, dream and reality fused together and she went rigid from head to foot.

'I said, get up.' He was scowling down at her, his voice crackling with static electricity. 'There's work to be done.'

Where was the tenderness of yesterday? her befuddled brain asked itself. But where, also, was that overwhelming passion? If that too was gone, well, she could almost welcome his ill-temper. She turned her head to see the clock.

'But it's only just gone six,' she protested.

'Too bad. The light's perfect.'

'Oh, damn the light—and damn you!'

Still overwrought from last night, her nerves were twanging now with anger. But then, as he jerked the sheet from her she flinched away, huddling herself into a little ball, and his lips tightened as he took in the instinctive movement.

'The light is perfect,' he repeated, his voice strangely remote all of a sudden. 'So I want to get out there and start painting.'

Their eyes met in a long, speaking glance, then she said sulkily, 'All right, slave-driver. Twenty minutes.'

'Ten.' And he turned on his heel.

'Twenty,' she yelled after him, and banged the pillow with her clenched fist.

Exactly a quarter of an hour later—she had decided finally to split the difference—she made her way into the kitchen, where Nik was just finishing a cup of coffee.

'About time.' His tone was caustic but she ignored him. 'Come on.' He uncoiled himself from his chair.

'For heaven's sake, I haven't had my breakfast yet,' she snapped.

'I thought women didn't eat breakfast these days.'

'Well, sorry, but *I* do,' she replied unsweetly, then very deliberately pulled out a chair, sat down and poured herself a coffee. 'And, if you aren't careful, I shan't sit at all today,' she muttered into her plate.

'Sorry. I didn't quite catch that,' Nik said, with an icy control.

'Didn't you?' She helped herself to yogurt, trickling the rich golden honey over it in an intricate spider's web.

'Sweetheart——' her hand jerked slightly so that she dropped a blob of honey, ruining the pattern '—I don't care for my models turning temperamental on me. If you know what's good for you...'

He expelled a loud breath then raked his fingers through his hair.

'OK, Catherine, let's call a truce—at least, until I've finished this painting.'

'All right,' she said in a small voice. Chewing on her lip, she hesitated, then went on, fidgeting with her knife, 'But I really think it would be better if I—well, got a room in the village.'

'What's the matter, *koukla*?' Just for a second, the old, slanting smile flashed out. 'Don't you trust me?'

No, I don't—and I don't trust myself, either. The words danced on the end of her tongue, but somehow she caught them back.

'Of course I do,' she replied stiffly. 'But just in case you're in any doubt, there isn't going to be any repeat of——' she broke off, feeling the blush turn her cheeks as scarlet as the poppies in the vase beside her, then swallowed and went on defiantly '—of last night.'

'Ah.' He nodded, as though storing away an interesting item of information. 'But you were right, you know—in Greece, too, possession *is* nine-tenths of the law. If you move out, well——' he shook his head sorrowfully '—it would almost certainly be construed as an admission that your claim is worthless. A pity—I told you, I enjoy a fight with a beautiful, wilful woman.'

'My claim is *not* worthless, and you know that quite well,' she retorted mechanically. In her fear of being under the same roof as Nik—oh, not so much in the daylight hours, but when those bewitching, velvet evenings came, doing strange, terrifying things to her—she'd completely forgotten about their battle for the house. But she wasn't going to give in over that—for if she did, it might open the floodgates and sweep aside her resistance in every other way.

'Tonight is not our night.' That was what he'd said—with the unmistakable promise that there would be others that *would* be theirs... She swallowed down the lump of fear lodged in her throat. Need she really worry, though? Last night, Nik had shown that he wasn't the kind of man to force himself physically on her. In his arrogance, he assumed that finally she'd give in to him without a struggle, so all that she had to do was keep saying no...no...no...

'I'm glad that's settled,' he said smoothly, then began opening cupboard doors. 'We'll take a picnic. It'll save coming back here at lunchtime.'

Catherine watched as he fetched out a bottle of wine, peaches, bread rolls and feta cheese, then started preparing a salad. Cucumber and tomatoes, spring onions, olives and fresh herbs—all were chopped, quickly and efficiently, then tipped into a bowl to join the rest of the meal in a lidded wicker basket.

Nik's hands were beautifully cared for—she found herself looking at them as if for the first time. Strange—they didn't at all look the hands of a man who rode and maintained motorbikes, who milked goats, who probably had to resort to any manual work he could find when his paintings didn't sell.

They were beautiful hands—strong and tanned. She saw them again, roving over her body, dark against light, the sea surging around them—until the moonlight had flickered on Julian's ring and she'd remembered... The stiletto-point of guilt twisted inside her again, and she vowed silently, fiercely, I'll never let it happen again. *Never*.

Down in the grove, she gathered another bunch of flowers while Nik prepared his gear, then he arranged her in the same pose as before. Finally, frowning critically, he sat back on his heels. His shorts were very brief; she could see his thighs, the sinews and muscles tense as he braced to balance himself. There was a faint sprinkling of dark hairs across the skin, thicker where they disappeared under the denim, towards his inner thighs...

'What the hell have you done to your hair?' He tugged at the offending strands until she winced.

'It got wet last night——' her eyes met his in shared memory, then slid away '—and I didn't have time to shampoo it this morning—remember?' Her overwrought state made it easy to inject acid into the word. 'I'll go and wash it if you like.'

'No, don't bother,' he grunted. 'It'll have to do.' He pulled the strands into place, then went back to his easel. 'OK, let's have the same expression.'

No, she wouldn't—she would not allow those treacherous images into her mind any more. But then, as Nik glowered at her and tapped his brush warningly against his thigh, she gave in, surrendering herself once again to the flowers, the scents and the overpowering magic of the place...

From beneath her lashes, Catherine sneaked another glance across the table at Nik. There was no need at all to be furtive though—he was staring down at the bleached pine wood as he had done for most of dinner, a morose scowl darkening his handsome face.

She sighed inwardly. All day she'd been treated to yet another, till now quite unsuspected facet of Nik's complex personality—moody, unpredictable, just plain difficult. Her lips tightened as she remembered the storm she'd brought down on herself by daring to move her badly cramped foot half an inch. After that particular exhibition of masculine bad temper, she'd hardly dared breathe.

Flick, flick. If he went on two minutes longer flicking his coffee spoon against his saucer, she'd leap up, snatch it out of his hand and—and hurl it into the tangle of roses climbing around the veranda. Flick—he looked up, met her eyes and, pushing his chair back, abruptly got to his feet.

'Where are you going?'

'To get on with my work, of course.'

'You mean—my portrait?'

'What else?'

'But—you've done so much at it today already.' And you look so tired and strained. She couldn't say that, though. 'Wouldn't it be better to start again fresh——?' Her voice tailed away as he favoured her with another scowl.

'I assume you want to take it for your precious Julian when you leave?' When she stared up blankly at him he went on, his voice even more abrasive. 'You've got just two weeks' leave from your bank—remember? From what I know of banks, they run on extremely well-ordered lines. I don't suppose it would do much for an assistant accounts manager's future prospects to play hookey on a Greek island. It might create entirely the wrong impression.' The sarcasm rasped on her flayed nerve-endings. 'Besides, what would dear Julian have to say, I wonder?'

'I've told you, just leave Julian out of this, will you?' Catherine slapped the flat of her hand down on the table.

'Gladly.' A pause. 'I'd be interested to meet him, though—if only to see the direction your—er—tastes run.'

Somehow she fixed a disdainful smile into place. 'I'm not going to react, Nik. Just because you've been in a foul mood all day, don't think you can get rid of your hang-ups by needling me. Your insults leave me cold, I'm afraid.'

'Cold?' His lips curled into a sneer. 'I couldn't have put it better myself, my sweet. Yes——' he went on reflectively, as her fingers bunched into angry little fists '—I'd quite like to see the kind of man you consider an appropriate marriage partner—in bed, as well as out of it.'

'I don't have to listen to this.' She leapt up, shoving back her chair with such violence that it tottered and fell with a crash, then pushed past him and went to her room.

When she reappeared a few minutes later he had gone and, her temper still sizzling almost audibly, Catherine strode off down the track. Tonight though, even the placid, imperturbable sound of the wind in the olive trees failed to calm her ruffled temper.

At the taverna, she slipped past the crowd of tourists at the bar and shut herself in the tiny international telephone booth she had noticed the previous evening. She leaned against the door, forcing herself to breathe slowly and steadily, until finally at least some of her twitching nerve-ends had smoothed themselves down again.

As she put her hand on the receiver, though, she hesitated, gnawing on her lower lip. She really ought to ring Julian—she'd promised him she would. But, still raw and emotionally bruised from a day on the receiving end of Nik's evil temper—and, far more, from that humiliating scene down on the beach last night—she couldn't face *his* anger. And he was going to be very angry, she knew that. No, she'd ring her parents instead, tell them, and the news would reach him fast enough.

Even so, the thought of their reaction made her groan inwardly, but then she set her soft mouth in a firm line. Her decision, which she'd been slowly coming to all day, *was* the right one, and no one was going to make her change her mind. She hadn't told Nik, though—the bitter thought of the gleam of triumph which would light up his dark eyes had kept her silent.

She was connected quickly—too quickly, for she was still enmeshed in her thoughts when her mother's clear voice broke in.

'Mum. It's Catherine.'

'Hello, dear. How are you?'

In the tiny, fly-spotted mirror just in front of her, she caught sight of dark shadows beneath her eyes, her face very pale, with something of that same tautness which Nik had had all day. Maybe it was contagious, like influenza. 'Oh, I'm fine, thank you.'

'And what about the villa? No problem, I hope.'

'Well, not exactly——' she began to hedge.

'You'll have to keep your foot behind that Greek lawyer, you know. They're all the same—the *mañana* complex, especially when they're dealing with a slip of a girl. I told you, you should have let your father or Julian come out there with you instead of——'

'No, Mum, everything's fine.' Catherine took a deep breath. 'The thing is, though, that——'

'Anyway, I expect you'd like to speak to Julian now.'

'Julian?' she echoed stupidly.

'Yes, of course, dear.' Her mother gave her tinkling little laugh. 'You've forgotten, haven't you? It's Thursday—Julian's here playing bridge with us and Dr Winterton. I'll fetch him.'

'No—please, don't.' Catherine almost dropped the phone. 'Look—there's something I have to tell you.'

'But Catherine——' her mother's voice rose in an outraged squawk '—you can't mean it. Look, you must speak to Julian, before you do anything foolish. You *must* be guided by him. I'll——'

'No—I can't. I-I've run out of drachmas.' A barefaced fib. 'I'll ring again on—what's today?' She pressed a finger to her throbbing temple. Oh, yes, Thursday night—bridge night. 'I'll ring on Sunday. Bye, love to everybody.'

She put the receiver down on her mother's heated protests then stood, leaning her head in her hand for a moment, before pushing open the door.

When she got back to the house, all the lights seemed to be on but there was no sight nor sound of Nik. He must have gone to bed, leaving them on for her. Silently she went through the house, switching them off as she went, but then, passing the half-open door of his studio, she stopped. He was there, his back to her, working at his easel. Beside him, on a table, was a tape recorder, playing

very softly—Basin Street Blues, the husky female
voice dark as bitter chocolate.

He was totally absorbed, as usual, so it was quite
safe to stand in the doorway, watching him, taking
in the way his thatch of black hair was in need of
a cut, the way one strand curled into his nape so
that she longed to twirl it round her finger and see
it spring back, yearned to cradle that dark head
between her breasts, feel again that warm, greedy
mouth suckle her.

Beneath her blouse, her nipples stirred and sprang
into life, and looking down she saw with horror
their outline, engorged and taut against the thin
cotton. She was turning away in blind confusion,
when Nik swung round.

'What do you want?'

He made no effort to come to her but, terrified
of what he might see, she instinctively flung up an
arm across her chest.

He muttered something under his breath—Greek,
but obviously highly unpleasant. Then, 'I said,
what do you *want*?'

After those unnerving sensations, his coiled anger
was like a stinging blow across her face. Just for a
second, she was tempted to run back to the phone
and tell her mother that she'd had second thoughts,
had seen sense after all. But no—not even Nik in
his foulest mood would change her decision.

'Can I see it?' Her eyes strayed past him in the
direction of the painting.

'Are you stupid or what?' he snarled. 'I've told you, *no, you can't.*'

'I-I'll go to bed, then.'

'You do that. Well?' as she continued to gaze at him, her body still snared by the spell of those tumultuous feelings. But finally she turned away and he began slapping paint on the canvas with his palette knife once again.

As they swept into the final bend Catherine clung on, one arm round Nik, the other clutching the bag of provisions. Just ahead, Ariadne and Persephone scampered into the trees, the bells round their necks jingling with indignation, but she barely saw them.

It had clouded over by mid-afternoon, so Nik, still with a black dog of a mood on both shoulders, had flung down his brush and called it a day. He'd announced that they'd eat in this evening, so they'd been down to the mini-market. A young English couple had been there, shopping together—they were obviously on a self-catering holiday—and under cover of going round the shelves she had watched them, even helped them at one point to locate the yogurts, before turning back as Nik asked her brusquely if she wanted cold sliced meat or frozen king-sized prawns for dinner.

'Prawns, I think,' she'd said. 'I know a very good recipe—sort of vaguely Chinese.' He'd actually creased his face in a slight smile at that. 'So you can work in your studio if you want, while I prepare it.'

And then she'd caught herself up with a little gasp. She was actually enjoying this shopping trip with Nik, and now they were talking exactly like that other couple, just as if they too were married... The thought had been deeply disquieting, giving her a peculiar little jolt in the pit of her stomach.

Nik braked hard, got off the bike and took the bag from her, setting it on the ground. Then, before she could climb down, he lifted her off in his arms and smiled down at her, his mood completely altered, in one of those mercurial changes she was becoming used to.

As she clung to him, still giddy from the crazy swoop up the winding track, his hands tightened on her waist.

'Catherine,' he said huskily.

'W-what?'

He gave her a lopsided smile. 'Nothing. Just—Catherine.'

Lifting his hand, he brushed the tangle of hair off her brow. But then all at once his eyes went past her face, and his fingers stilled.

'Well, well,' he drawled. 'It appears, *koukla mou*, that we have company.'

Catherine swung round just as the man, who had been sitting in one of the upright chairs on the veranda, got up and came to stand at the top of the steps. She stared at him in utter disbelief, and then the single word came out as a strangled croak.

'*Julian!*'

CHAPTER EIGHT

'HELLO, Catherine.' His voice was chill and, when he made no move towards her, Nik gestured her past him with an ironic sweep of his hand.

Catherine, feeling ever so slightly sick, went up the steps, instinctively putting up a hand to smooth her untidy hair. Julian was angry, very angry—his normally pale face was flushed and his mouth was compressed into a tight line.

Suddenly, horribly conscious of a pair of sardonic dark blue eyes taking in every detail of this lovers' reunion, she desperately wanted him to crush her in his arms and smother her with fiancé-like kisses. But as she smiled tentatively and turned her face up, Julian merely brushed her cheek in the coolest of greetings, and she took a step back.

'What a wonderful surprise, darling.' Her rapture, though, sounded thin even to her own ears. 'But what on earth are you doing here?'

'I should have thought that was obvious,' he said coldly. 'After your extraordinary phone call last night, your parents were naturally very concerned about you, so although I had an important meeting scheduled for this afternoon——' she finally registered his totally out of place pinstripe suit and neat tie '—I had to drop everything and catch this morning's flight.'

'But there was no need.' She felt a spurt of irritation. Her father and Julian had both tried to insist that she couldn't possibly deal with her grandfather's will herself, and now, at the first sign of trouble, one of them was out here.

'It seems to me there was *every* need,' he replied tartly.

Before she could reply, she became aware of Nik behind her, holding the bag of groceries.

'I'll take these through to the kitchen, Catherine.' He gave Julian the briefest of glances. 'You'll stay to dinner, of course.'

Julian eyed him, taking in with obvious distaste the ancient T-shirt, scuffed trainers and sawn-off jeans, then turned back to her. 'Perhaps you'll introduce me, darling.'

'Oh, yes, of course—sorry,' she said, flustered. 'Julian, this is Nik—Nik Demetrios. Nik, meet Julian Grey, my fiancé.'

'Delighted to meet you, Julian,' Nik drawled, with patent insincerity. 'Catherine's told me so much about you.'

As she shot him a baleful look, the two men shook hands perfunctorily.

'You live on Skiathos, do you?' Julian enquired stiffly.

Nik gave an amiable smile, which showed his perfect white teeth and made Catherine want to kick him—hard—on the shin. 'That's right.'

'And you're a neighbour of Catherine's, are you?'

'Well, not exactly,' and, even as she shot him an imploring look, he added, 'I live here.'

'Oh, I'm sorry. There must be some mistake.' Julian turned back to Catherine. 'Have I come to the wrong house? The taxi driver seemed——'

'No,' Nik cut in suavely, 'there's no mistake. This is the Villa Angelika.'

Julian's eyes narrowed, going from one to the other of them. 'But I don't——'

'Look, darling,' she said hastily, 'it-it's all very complicated. Let's sit down, and I'll explain.'

'Right, I'll put these things away,' Nik said briskly. 'Fancy a drink, either of you? Tea perhaps?' But his innocuous smile did not fool her for an instant, and she glared at him.

'Not just now, thank you,' Julian replied, so Nik nodded and, whistling tunelessly between his teeth, headed off into the house. As she lowered herself down on to a chaise-longue, Catherine expelled a silent sigh of relief—at least he'd had the tact to take himself off while she did her best to sort things out.

'Now,' Julian sat back down in his upright chair, 'perhaps you'll be good enough to tell me just what's going on.'

'About Nik—living here, you mean?'

'Among other things, yes. Such as, where you're staying.'

'Well,' she felt the rosy colour seep into her cheeks, 'actually I'm living here as well.'

'I see.' The temperature on the veranda dropped to freezing.

'No, you don't.' Her voice rose vehemently.

'Oh, come on darling.' His lips curled derisively. 'You expect me to believe that you're here alone—I take it that you two are alone?'

'Well, yes,' she agreed reluctantly. 'But——'

'And that he——' he jerked a thumb in the direction of the door '—hasn't so much as made a pass at you?'

'Julian!' Her face was flaming now.

'These over-sexed Greek tomcats—they're all the same.'

'Oh, what utter nonsense!' She forced a shaky laugh. 'But even if he had, I'm engaged to you, aren't I?' Even as she spoke, though, the image rose in her mind of that warm night at the sea's edge, of herself, naked and trembling in Nik's arms, and as the guilty shame pierced her like a knife-blade she leapt up precipitately. 'Are you sure you wouldn't like a drink?'

'Quite sure.' And as, reluctantly, she sat down again, 'You still haven't explained what he's doing here.'

'Well, you see he was already here when I arrived.'

'A squatter!' Julian's handsome face tightened. 'Really, Catherine—why haven't you just got rid of him?'

'But it's not quite as simple as that.'

'Of course it is. All these freeloaders need is a firm hand taken to them—and if you won't, I will. Where's the nearest police station?'

'No! I've told you—it's all highly complicated.' She cleared her throat. 'He-he's disputing my claim to the house.'

'What?' Julian's jaw dropped. 'But he can't.'

'I'm afraid I can.' Nik, a glass of ouzo in hand, had appeared in the doorway, and as Catherine, hands clenched, watched him, he sauntered across to lean against the veranda rail.

'Perhaps you'd kindly enlighten me as to the grounds for your assertion?' As Julian's voice took on its clipped, professional tone, she saw the two men take the measure of each other, and simultaneously she realised that each loathed what he saw.

'Simply this,' Nik said coolly. 'My father won the villa in a wager with Catherine's grandfather.'

'A wager!' Julian laughed scornfully. 'You expect me to believe that? And just what evidence do you have for this—wager?'

'The playing card, properly signed and witnessed by a fellow customer at the taverna.'

'The taverna! I might have guessed. And no doubt he was stoned out of his mind at the time on cheap Greek booze.'

Catherine's nails bit into her hands. 'I'm sure he wasn't, Julian.'

'Oh, come now, Catherine. The drunken old reprobate——' she fought down the sudden surge of anger '—sorry, darling, but we both know that he was—was no doubt made so incapable that he didn't know what he was doing. This will be a major plank of our case if this ever comes to court.'

It was almost word for word what she'd said to Nik, but somehow to hear Julian say it rasped on her inflamed nerves.

'And what have you been doing about all this nonsense?' he demanded.

'Well, we—that is, I,' she amended hastily, 'have been to see Mr Joannides, Grandfather's lawyer.'

'And what did he have to say?'

'Actually,' she hesitated, conscious of the inevitable reaction, 'he thinks there might be something in the claim.'

Julian's lip curled. 'Well, of course he would, wouldn't he? A Greek will always look after a Greek.'

Out of the corner of her eye, she saw Nik's hands bunch into fists at his side, and for a terrifying moment thought that he was about to advance on Julian. The two men were much of a height and build, but she was under no illusion as to who would be stretched out on the wooden boards of the veranda in ten seconds flat. But even as she went rigid with tension, Nik's fists uncurled.

'Don't concern yourself on that score,' he said levelly. 'Stavros Joannides is Catherine's lawyer, not mine, and he is wholly trustworthy in all his professional dealings.'

She relaxed a fraction. Thank heavens that for a Greek, a visitor—a guest—was almost sacred, and whatever the provocation, Nik would never have hit him.

No, a clear little voice whispered in her ear, but if he ever feels the need, he'll choose other, more subtle, Byzantine means to exact his revenge.

'It seems to me, darling——' Julian chose to ignore Nik's last remark '—that you've completely mishandled the situation from the start. And as for that incoherent telephone call last night—if only you hadn't hung up before I had a chance to speak to you——' looking quickly at Nik she saw his dark brows rise fractionally '—I could have talked you out of this ridiculous idea of giving up our development plans.'

Nik's eyes went from Julian to her and for a moment his blue-black gaze locked with hers. But she could not read his expression—he was far too accomplished a poker player for that.

'Even to consider that would be to play completely into the hands of——' Julian paused, as though searching for a suitable epithet '—the opposition.'

'But you won't feel that way, not once you've seen the olive groves and the flower meadow,' she said earnestly. 'Come on down with me, and I'll show you—now.' Apart from anything else, she was desperate to get away from that shuttered, ironic pair of eyes, which missed nothing and yet at the same time gave nothing away.

'Very well.' His tone was grudging. 'But change first, darling—that T-shirt does nothing for you. Oh, and do put your hair up. You look like a——'

'She looks like a dryad—a woodland nymph,' Nik interposed softly, and they both jerked round to him.

Julian scowled, and Catherine, horribly conscious of the tensions crackling just beneath the surface of the triangle between them, said hastily, 'Yes, all right. I won't be a minute.' And without another glance at either of the two men, she hurried indoors.

As she crossed the sitting-room, though, she came face to face with her reflection in the harem mirror, and pulled up sharply. Julian was right—she did look a mess, her pale fudge-coloured hair hanging in untidy strands round her flushed face. Not at all the usual poised, immaculately turned out Catherine Turner, bank manager in the making.

And that T-shirt—another impulse buy and far too big, so that it would keep slipping off one shoulder, as it was now, to reveal an expanse of delicately tanned skin. 'She looks like a dryad...' She gazed at herself a moment longer, her full lips parting tremulously, then abruptly wrenched up the shirt once more and turned away.

In her bedroom, she grabbed her housecoat and went across to the bathroom to shower. The water was deliciously cool against her overheated skin, but she only let herself stay a couple of minutes. As she was patting herself dry though, her nostrils caught the faint, elusive scent of sandalwood. Nik's aftershave—he must have forgotten to screw on the cap. But when she opened the cabinet, there was the bottle, tightly closed, and she slammed the door again. Damn him! His presence was taking over the entire house, so that she was never free of him ...

Back in her room, she brushed her hair and, for speed, caught it into a smooth pony-tail, then opened the wardrobe and took out an outfit which she knew Julian liked—a white cotton shirt and a skirt in soft blue and brown Madras checks.

As she closed her door, she heard a faint murmur of voices coming not from the veranda but from further along the passage. When she paused in the doorway of Nik's studio, the two men were standing in front of the easel at the far end.

'Ah, Catherine.' Their backs were to her, but Nik must have heard her. 'I was just showing Julian some of my work,' he said easily.

With a strange sense of foreboding, she went up to them, then saw with relief that the picture on the easel was a seascape.

'Yes, very nice.' Julian was being extra-polite, but she knew that wildly swirling, dark blue-green waves crashing down in white foam were not his style at all.

'Here's another.' Nik hooked the seascape off the easel and replaced it with a view of Skiathos Town and the harbour. 'I reckon I'll find a wealthy tourist for this one. Don't you think so, Catherine?'

His eyes were sardonic, mocking not only her, but subtly Julian as well. 'I'm sure you will,' she replied woodenly.

'Oh, and you'll be interested in this one, Julian. It's not quite finished, but——'

'No!' Catherine knew suddenly which painting he meant, but Nik only smiled blandly at her.

'Oh, sorry. Were you keeping it as a surprise? But surely a man ought to know what he's getting for a wedding present?' And he set her portrait on the easel.

It was the first time she had seen it and she stared at it, her eyes wide. It was beautiful, the silvery olive trees in the background, the flowers around her echoing those in her lap, the folds of her skirt and yes—finally, she dared look at herself—such a good likeness, though she certainly wasn't that pretty. But after all, didn't all portrait painters flatter!

'I think I've captured something of the essential Catherine—although that's a very elusive quality, of course. Don't you agree, Julian?'

'You think so?' At his tone, she looked up at him and saw a faint flush on his cheekbones.

'But—don't you like it?' she faltered. 'I think it's lovely.'

'No—I'm sorry, darling. It was a nice thought, but——' he turned back to Nik '—I think not.'

'Why ever not?' she asked, bewildered. 'What's wrong with it?'

'Well, for a start—where's your engagement ring?'

She looked blankly at him. 'What do you mean?'

'I should have thought that if it was intended as a wedding present, you'd have been wearing your ring.'

She swung round to the painting. He was right—her right hand was hidden among the flowers, but her left lay across her thigh—bare of any ring.

'Sorry, I must have overlooked it!' Nik's voice was velvet-smooth, but meeting that expressionless gaze, she was perfectly certain that the omission was deliberate.

'But is that the only reason?' she demanded. 'I'm sure Nik will paint it in. Won't you?' But his only response was the faintest shrug, and Julian was going on, as if she hadn't spoken.

'I shall be happy, of course, Demetrios, to reimburse you for your time.'

Just for a moment, she glimpsed a flash of contempt in those cool blue eyes, so searing that it should have shrivelled Julian to the bone. All Nik said though, was, 'I'm afraid my hourly rates come rather high. But, in any case, I'm sure I'll find another buyer easily enough.'

They couldn't do it—Julian reject the painting, Nik casually sell it to the first tourist who came along. Locked into their private battle of mutual antagonism across the top of her head, couldn't they both see that?

She stared at the painting, until it blurred and shimmered through a haze of tears, and felt a fierce surge of possessiveness sweep through her so that she wanted to snatch it off the easel and cradle it to her. No one else should have it—no one!

She blinked away the tears and turned to Julian. 'I thought I was supposed to be showing you the olive grove,' and she walked out, leaving him to follow.

'I forgot to ask,' she said stiffly as they made their way down the path, breaking a silence that had lasted several minutes, 'what have you done with your luggage?'

'It's back at the hotel, of course. I booked myself in there before coming on here.'

She stopped in surprise. 'But there's plenty of room in the villa.'

'I'm aware of that,' he said frigidly, 'but I had thought you'd rather I behaved properly. It seems I was wrong, though.'

'And just what do you mean by that?'

'Simply that you don't seem to share my sense of the proprieties.'

Catherine struggled to rein in her temper. 'I haven't s-slept with Nik, if that's what you mean. Apart from anything else, I'm engaged to you. But surely you wouldn't have wanted me to move out and leave him here on his own. You know what they say about nine-tenths of the law.'

'Yes, all right,' he replied testily. 'Let's get on, shall we?'

In the olive grove, she led the way across to the gnarled old tree. 'This is where my portrait was done. I was sitting up against this trunk.' She looked up at him. 'Do you really not like it, Julian? I know you've taken an instant aversion to Nik—and I can't say I blame you——' she managed a teasing smile '—but don't let that spoil it for you.'

'No, it's nothing to do with him—although it's just the kind of thing I'd expect him to come up with. If you must know, I don't care for a portrait where my wife is making bedroom eyes at any man who happens to look at it.'

'Bedroom eyes!' She stared at him blankly. 'I don't know what you mean.'

'Don't you? Take another look some time, then. Get past the chocolate box exterior, and it's positively indecent.'

'Indecent!' Her voice rose. 'But I'm fully dressed—not stretched out nude.' For a second the memory of Elena, lying back on the bed, slid across her mind.

'That's nothing to do with it,' Julian said frostily. 'Just look at the eyes—the whole expression on your face.'

'I'm sure you're wrong,' she said rather shakily. 'But even so, it was for you.'

'Was it?' His voice was grim. 'I wasn't around when it was painted.'

'No, but I was thinking of you.' It was a lie, of course—the face of the man who in her mind loomed over her as she lay naked in the grass had not been Julian's. 'Anyway,' she went on hurriedly, 'this is what I've brought you down to see.'

The evening sun was casting long shadows through the olives and into the flower meadow beyond, where Ariadne and Persephone were munching happily, their bells chiming faintly.

Julian looked around him and smiled. 'Yes, I see what you mean. We certainly mustn't destroy all this.'

Her heart lifted. 'So you do understand? It would——'

'This is a priceless asset. We'll have to get Stephen to take it into account in his plans, to retain as much of it as possible.'

'But——'

'I'm sure he'll be able to build round some of these trees, and if we have to bulldoze the flowers, well, we can reseed an area.'

'Bulldoze the flowers!' Catherine could barely get the words out for the pain in her chest. 'But I thought you understood. That would be desecration—any building here would be.'

Julian regarded her through narrowed eyes. 'Desecration? Is that your own word—or has someone been busy feeding it to you?'

'I—of course it is.' She took a deep breath, then looked at him steadily. 'We're not building here. This is my land—if I don't lose it, that is—and I won't have it destroyed, just for the sake of money.' She broke off, then gave him a conciliatory smile. 'It can be just for us—our holiday home. Perhaps we could honeymoon here?'

But he did not return her smile. 'I don't know what's happening to you, Catherine. You're just not the girl I'm engaged to. You're always so super-efficient at work.'

'Yes I am, aren't I?' she said, rather miserably.

'It's this place—it gets to people, it must do.' He ran his fingers through his brown hair. 'Your grandfather, that layabout up there—and now you. You've been out here—what?—less than a week, and you're falling apart already. You should be chasing up that lawyer, asking questions at the taverna—finding out how much that so-called witness was paid for his signature. And what have you been doing?' He expelled a long, exasperated breath. 'Sitting around having your portrait painted!'

Catherine's jaw tilted slightly. 'I'm perfectly capable of running my own affairs.'

'You think so?'

'And what do you suggest we do, then?' Her voice was dangerously quiet.

'Get our hands on that playing card, for a start. Without that, he's lost.'

'Destroy it, you mean?' She gaped at him. 'But that would be dishonest.'

Julian's laugh rasped on her. 'And you think that unscrupulous bastard wouldn't play dirty, if he got the chance? Open your eyes, darling—in our line of work, you should be a better judge of men than that.'

'No,' she exclaimed. 'Whatever else Nik is, he's straight—I'm sure of that.' Though why on earth she was acting as devil's advocate for one particular devil who was perfectly capable of looking after himself, she didn't know.

'Well, all I can say is that it's fortunate I've got out here in time. We'll go back to the villa now and you'll pack.'

'But why?'

'You're not spending another night out here— I'll get you a room in my hotel. Tomorrow we'll see this lawyer—no, on second thoughts, I'll see him on my own, get some action out of him. For a start, have an eviction order served on——' he jerked his thumb towards the villa and Nik '—and then tomorrow afternoon we're flying home.'

'Now wait a——'

'The sooner you're back in England, the better. What you need is a cold douche of common sense.'

Catherine looked at him for a long, long moment. Strange—what had drawn her to Julian from the start had been his dynamic, incisive mind, the feeling that he would always know what he wanted, and get it. So different from Nik Demetrios—who was everything she didn't admire in a man...

At last she spoke. 'I'm sorry, Julian, but I'm not coming into town, and I'm not going back to England with you. I'm not going ahead with the development and——' she spoke almost as if it was an afterthought, and gave him a sad, blurred little smile '—I'm very sorry, but I'm not going to marry you.'

CHAPTER NINE

THE portrait was still on the easel. Catherine walked slowly across and stood gazing at it. Julian had been right, of course, she thought drearily—and so had that inner voice of warning. By showing him the painting, Nik had chosen the subtlest way possible of exacting his revenge.

It was there for anyone to see—only she herself had been too naïve. The warmly rounded, living—loving—flesh; the way she lay back against the tree, her eyes half closed, every limb relaxed and heavy with a drowsy sensuality. Catherine stared into those eyes, strange, disquieting sensations churning over and over in her stomach.

'He's gone, then?' The softly spoken words made her swing round to see Nik leaning in the doorway.

'Of course he's gone.' She'd stayed for what seemed like hours in the olive grove, struggling for some kind of composure, and then, at the sight of Nik, propped up, arms folded casually, the composure splintered. 'What do you expect? After all, that was what you intended all along, wasn't it?'

'Was it?' He straightened up and came across to her.

'You know very well it was.' Her voice shook slightly. 'You took an instant dislike to him and——'

'I'd say the feeling was fairly mutual.'

'And you decided to make as much trouble as you could. You brought him in here deliberately, knowing how he'd react.'

'Yes, I'm sorry about the ring.'

'No, you're not.' She almost spat the words. 'You left it out on purpose. But I'm not talking about the ring, and you know it. You knew that Julian would see—even if I was too stupid——' her voice trembled at his treachery '—what was in it.'

'And what did he see that so upset him?'

'That horrible expression.' Unable to look at the painting, she waved an angry hand at it. 'You-you've imposed someone else on it. You've——' She stopped abruptly, her mouth slightly open, and forced herself to turn towards the easel then back to him. 'You've painted Elena instead of me. My face, but her expression. You were thinking of her all the time, that little——'

'*Isiho*.' Nik laid his hand to her mouth, and the unexpected gesture silenced her. 'I was not thinking of Elena, or anyone else, when I painted you.'

She jerked her head back. 'And just how do you expect me to believe that?'

'Simply because I could not possibly have been aware of any other woman while you were in front of me.' There was a look in his eyes, which made her drop her own in confusion. 'This painting is of you, Catherine—it's the finest portrait I have ever done.'

Well, why are you going to sell it to the first tourist with money, then? The thought wrenched at her, but she bit her lip hard to stem the flood tide of tears she felt within her.

'I painted nothing that is not there.' His voice was inexorable. 'As I told Julian, I have caught the essential, inner woman, with all her secret, sensual thoughts.'

And at his words, she saw herself in the olive grove again, lying naked among the flowers, saw the face of the man bending towards her. It slid like a transparency across the features of the man standing opposite her—slid, then jelled into position. It was Nik who'd leaned towards her in that waking dream, his hand reaching out to—Catherine gave a choked little whimper and dragged herself free of the treacherous miasma.

'That's a lie,' she burst out wildly. 'It isn't there. I'm not like that—not at all. J-Julian saw that.'

'Oh, no, my sweet. It is precisely because he did see it—for the very first time, for a man like that could never have found it himself——' his lip curled slightly '—and did not like what he saw, that he rejected the portrait. And you.'

'No, that's not true. I'm not like that, I tell you.' Her mouth quivered.

'Oh, *koukla mou*, don't.'

Nik went to take her in his arms, but at the sudden tenderness in his voice her overwrought nerves finally twanged a hair's breadth too much and snapped.

She thrust him away. 'Leave me alone, damn you. Julian—you—I've had enough!'

And, flinging a hand to her mouth, she pushed blindly past him, ran headlong out of the studio, and out of the house.

Down in the grove she halted to lean against the trunk of an olive tree—her tree, where Nik had painted her, though she was barely aware of that. She stayed there, her lungs sobbing for breath after that wild rush down the hillside, until she saw, advancing purposefully through the trees towards her, Nik. Why couldn't he see that she wanted—needed—to be alone? Springing upright, she made a bolt for it.

'Catherine!' His tone was half-amused, half-exasperated.

'Go away,' she flung over her shoulder, then felt his hands go round her waist. 'Oh!'

She tried to pull away, tripped over a tree root half out of the ground and went sprawling, bringing Nik down with her so that he fell across her, winding her completely. She lay, half stunned, her face buried in a clump of poppies, the arm she had flung up to save herself crushing a root of yellow daisies. Then Nik's weight lifted from her and his hands were on her shoulders, dragging her half upright.

'*Gatali*, are you all right?' But the concern mingled with wicked laughter in his voice, and suddenly her fury erupted.

'Of course I'm not all right. You-you——' she was still fighting for breath '—I told you to leave me alone.'

Brushing her hair off her face, she glowered up at him with impotent rage, then all at once saw the laughter die from his eyes. His fingers, which had been resting lightly on her shoulders, tightened to bite into her flesh, and with an incoherent sound deep in his throat he dragged her into his arms.

His mouth came down on hers, scorching it, sending red-gold flames licking through her whole body until she was on fire, while the velvet shaft of his tongue alternately caressed and thrust against the length of hers so that her mouth was filled with the sweetness of him, and her nostrils with the aroma of sun-warmth and sweat.

When one hand took her full breast, cupping it, she felt the heat of his palm sear her flesh through the cotton shirt, and her nipple hardened to press against his gently stroking thumb as hot tides washed through her, each more scalding than the one before.

The forest fire had all but engulfed her, but she couldn't succumb—she mustn't.

'No, Nik,' she gasped into his mouth. 'No.'

But he ensnared the breathless little sigh. 'Yes, Catherine—yes.'

Running his moist lips down the column of her throat, he fastened on the crazy pulse at its base, gently teasing at it with his tongue, tasting her, until a gasp was torn from her and she arched her neck against him, her eyes closing as her head fell back against his arm.

His free hand left her breast and slid down, moulding his palm to the lush curve of her waist and thighs. She felt him ease her skirt aside and then that searching hand brushed across her stomach, slowly so that she could feel the pulse at the base of his thumb beat against her skin. Then it slid inside her cotton panties, the outspread fingers resting possessively across the warm flesh at the very apex of her trembling thighs.

In an instinctive movement, she closed her legs against him. 'No.'

'Ssssh.' His mouth was against her throat. 'It's all right, my sweet.' Again, that infinitesimal movement of his fingers, the sensation rippling out to every part of her.

'Nik?' she whispered tremulously, and he shushed her again like a child.

'Don't be afraid. Trust me, *agape mou.*'

As her legs lost their tautness he began softly stroking her, his fingertip lost in the satiny folds, moving gently to and fro until a rhythm began to build in her, overwhelming in its intensity. Gradually, under that fingertip caress, she was losing all control, hurtling irretrievably towards something—she didn't know what. Her eyes, which had been closed, opened and she gazed blindly up at him.

'Nik?' She was pleading for reassurance, and he smiled down at her, a smile of such tenderness that all her fears melted like snow in the warmth of spring.

'It's all right,' he repeated softly. 'I would never hurt you, little one. So—don't fight it any more.'

He eased his finger a fraction nearer her molten centre, and instantly the flames leapt up and devoured her as her hips arched out of control against him. Just for a second, her entire body went rigid before that incandescent centre exploded, shooting white-hot sparks of fire, then it slowly subsided, leaving her inert and leaden-limbed.

Nik gently stroked the sweat-soaked hair from her face, smiling down at her. All at once though, she could not meet his eye and turned her head away in confusion, but he tilted her face back towards him.

'Don't be shy, my sweet. We've been friends too long for that.'

She stared up at him, and without warning all the tensions and traumas of the day, coupled with that marvellous, terrifying sensation which had all but destroyed her, were suddenly too much for her. She clapped the back of her hand to her mouth, biting fiercely on it in an effort to stem first the slow tears and then the sobs which racked her.

Gently yet firmly Nik removed her hand. 'If you want to bite something, try my shoulder for size,' he said, and, torn between a laugh and a sob, she turned her face into his chest as he gathered her to him and held her, one hand softly stroking her hair.

At last the tears stopped and she eased herself away. 'Sorry about that.' She managed a watery smile. 'It's been quite a day.'

He took her left hand and turned it over, looking at that circle of paler skin on her empty finger, then suddenly crushed it in his.

'Was it too awful, *koukla*?'

'No. Y-yes.'

Her voice wobbled dangerously as she remembered Julian's angry, disbelieving face, then the outpouring of coldly vicious words which had severed her very heartstrings. There was a crushed poppy lying beside her. She picked it up, running her fingernail up and down the rough stem.

'It took him some time to realise that I meant it,' she said at last.

'How did you convince him?'

'I told him——' her face was lowered, screened by her hair, so that he had to bend to hear her words '—in the end, I told him that I know now that I can never marry a bank manager.'

'I see. Not even a rich, up and coming one?' There was an odd little note in Nik's voice, but when she glanced up his eyes held only a teasing warmth.

'You were right.' Her voice was still strained. 'You said I could never be happy with one.'

'Well——' he pulled a face '—I don't think I exactly said that. But it's over now, so don't fret about it any more.' A crooked little smile. 'We have far more important things to think about tonight.'

'Such as?' She looked up at him at last from beneath her lashes.

'Such as this, my sweet.'

And, very deliberately, he began undoing the buttons on her shirt. He peeled it off her then unhooked her bra, pulling it away so that her breasts fell softly against his hands, and she heard his breath expelled in a faint hiss.

'You are lovely—so very lovely,' he said softly, then, unzipping her skirt, slipped it down over her legs to leave her just in her panties.

Putting her hand on his chest, she felt the thunderous heartbeat beneath her fingers, and as he caught the hem of his T-shirt she murmured, 'Let me.'

She peeled it off him, slowly so that first the flat, horizontally ridged muscles of his tanned stomach came into view, then his chest, with its dark scattering of hairs, and finally the strong length of his throat. He shook his head to pull it clear of the shirt, then shrugged himself out of his shorts.

Catherine bit her lip. 'Oh, Nik,' she whispered. 'You're so—beautiful.'

He was. So beautifully, proudly masculine—just as on the beach that moonlit night, but while then he'd been a silver statue, now he was warm, living flesh and blood.

He laid her among the flowers, their stems tickling her bare skin, then finally slid off her panties and, propping himself on one elbow, ran his hand over her body. As it trembled under his touch, he lowered his head and caught first one then the other rosy nipple in his mouth, tantalising them, playing with them until the erotic intensity made her writhe to and fro, helpless in his grasp.

'Nik.' Her hands tangled in his hair, her nails raking his scalp as he drew her to him so that they formed that most perfect and timeless of symmetries, all yielding curves and hard-planed angles. Burying his tongue in her mouth, he thrust into her soft sweetness in a mime of the thrust of his pelvis against hers.

Deep inside her, like some inland sea, dark tides were moving, slowly yet inexorably catching her up in a relentless surge. She moaned, a deep, primal sound of hunger, and Nik answered it by moving over her. Then, as her legs parted to receive him, he entered her in one long, slow movement.

Just for a moment, her muscles contracted against this first invasion. Then, as he filled her with his potent force, beginning to move in a slow, sensuous rhythm, she could only cling to him, her fingers digging into his shoulders as though he were a lifeline for her, to brace her against that dark tide which was coursing through her, sweeping her away on its flood waters.

The sweet slide of flesh against flesh increased in tempo, until the world faded away and she could feel nothing beyond that wild, uncontrollable ecstasy. And then the running tide finally snatched her out of the safety of Nik's embrace, before flinging her down, spent and lifeless as a piece of driftwood, on a distant shore.

Next instant Nik, his whole body slippery with sweat, raised himself slightly to look down at her, his eyes black and glittering as though with fever, then collapsed on her...

His arm lay heavily across her. Catherine's eyes fluttered then opened to see the midnight-blue velvet sky above them, and she turned her head slightly, to see Nik lying on his side. His face was a pale blur against the black and grey of the meadow and trees, but she saw his eyes glint, obsidian dark.

'Hi,' he said softly, and, lifting a lazy hand, brushed his fingers across her mouth.

'Hi.' As she smiled rather tremulously at him he sat up, pulling her up with him. She leaned against his broad chest, her head resting in the crook of his shoulder as he rubbed his cheek across her hair, his chin catching in the strands. He needs a shave, she thought, with a little stab of tenderness.

The air around them was heavy with perfume. 'Mmmm, what a wonderful smell,' she murmured. 'Honeysuckle, I suppose.'

'Yes, there's one climbing up this olive. Keep still.' Reaching across, he snapped a flower and tucked it into her hair, just behind her ear, then nibbled gently at the lobe before whispering huskily, 'Let's go back to the house.'

Getting to his feet, he lifted her in his arms and began striding back through the grove.

'But I can walk,' she protested.

'Not tonight.'

He hoisted her higher to drop a kiss on her brow, then carried her up the track towards the villa as Catherine, feeling more secure than ever in her life before, lay back and closed her eyes.

She opened them as Nik paused in the passage.

'My room, I think,' he said, shouldering open his door.

'*Your* room?' She pouted up at him, her eyes alight with mischief. 'None of this house is yours—remember?'

The last word ended in a squeak as, without warning, he tossed her down onto his bed.

'No, I don't remember any such thing,' he growled and as Catherine, caught between laughter and terror, went to roll off the bed, he flung himself down across her.

The battle was brief—and very unequal—ending with her spreadeagled, her hair all over her face and both wrists trapped in one of his hands while the other, in spite of her frantic struggles, pinned her to the sheet.

'Now,' he grinned down at her wickedly, 'beg my forgiveness.'

'No, I won't.'

'Perhaps I should tell you what I'm going to do to you if you don't.'

'I don't care.' But the nervous laughter was bubbling up inside her.

'I'm going to ravish every inch of that wonderful body—very, very slowly.' His voice dropped to a low, throaty purr like a predatory leopard. 'I'm going to bring it to life, until it is hungry—no, greedy for everything I give it. Going to apologise?' he added casually.

'C-certainly not,' she gasped, and tensed to break his grip. But she was powerless, and could only lie there as he proceeded to carry out his threat.

His only weapons his skilled hands and mouth, he inexorably wooed and conquered her so that she forgot to struggle and lay helplessly writhing as time after time he deliberately brought her to the very brink of human existence then drew her back away from the precipice.

Naïvely, she had imagined that nothing could be more shattering than that ecstasy in the olive grove. Now though, under Nik's sensual assault, she felt something very deep inside her begin to stir, to unleash itself. It was, in a strange way, terrifying, and she fought it, knowing instinctively that if it came to life and flowered in her it could never be crushed again. She would have to live the rest of her life with this new inner self.

But it was too late. Under that relentless, erotic attack, her womanhood, her very core, leapt up like a burning flame. She reached blindly for Nik to pull him down to her, raising her hips for him, and she felt his sweetness fill her as the furnace of their passion consumed them both.

Hours later, it seemed, he lifted his head from where it had lain pillowed on her breast and gave her a lopsided smile.

'Catherine.' Taking her hand, he pressed his lips into the palm until her fingers curled around him. 'Don't think about the villa. This is—just us, not taking from each other but giving freely, joyfully sharing.'

And, clasped in each other's arms, together they fell into a bottomless sleep...

When Catherine finally roused, the room was filled with golden sunlight. Just for a moment, she lay languidly on her back, staring at the unfamiliar room, then memory came pouring back. She turned on her side to seek Nik's arms but he was not there. Instantly, she felt bereft, a desolate emptiness filling her, but even as her eyes smarted with sudden tears, the door opened and he appeared, wearing a navy robe and carrying a tray.

He set it down on the side table then sat on the edge of the bed and, taking her hand, carried it to his lips.

'*Kaliméra*, my little dove,' he said softly. 'Did you sleep well?'

'Mmmm.' She yawned and stretched voluptuously under the linen sheet, then smiled back at him, a sleepy cat's smile.

Nik's eyes darkened. 'You shouldn't smile at me like that.'

'Why not?' She looked up at him, her eyes wide and innocent.

Bending forward, he kissed one nipple then the other through the sheet, but as she gave a faint gasp he said, 'Because, *koukla*, it is breakfast-time, that is why not. Now, sit up.'

As he piled pillows behind her, she glanced at the tray for the first time.

'Oh—Nik.' Sparkling-eyed, she laughed, '*Champagne*?'

'Of course. What else on such a glorious morning?'

Taking the bottle of Dom Perignon out of the silver ice bucket by its neck, he extracted the cork with only the faintest pop, then poured the foaming straw-coloured nectar into two flutes and handed one to her.

'What shall we drink to?' He pursed his lips in thought. 'Oh, yes, let's drink to the present—forget tomorrow.'

'Yes,' she said quickly, to drown out that cold little voice in her ear. 'The present.'

They clinked glasses and she took a sip, feeling the bubbles prickle at her throat and mouth, still swollen from Nik's kisses.

'Hold out your glass.'

He took from a dish a fat ripe strawberry, dipped it into her champagne then popped it into her mouth, followed by another and another.

'I feel like Miss Universe.' Catherine lay back on her pillow with a sigh of utter contentment, and when he raised one brow enquiringly, 'Well, she's always in the papers, sitting up in bed drinking champagne the morning after she's won.'

'*Agape mou*——' over the rim of his glass, Nik's eyes met hers '—no Miss Universe was ever half so beautiful as you are at this moment.'

Taking the flute from her he set it down, then scooped her up into his arms and carried her through into the sitting-room, where he set her slowly down in front of the harem mirror.

'Now—what do you see?' he murmured in her ear, holding her close against him, his arms crossed over her breasts, so that she was achingly aware of his warm, vibrant body.

What did she see? And what had Nik said about this mirror—that it could see through you to the truth within? Almost fearfully, she looked at herself in the misty surface and saw her naked body, surely more rounded, more voluptuous than it had been yesterday, the skin gleaming like satin. But it was the face which really held her. Her cheeks glowed with a hectic brilliance, her lips—she ran the tip of her tongue around them—were parted as if to receive a lover's kiss, while her eyes——

'I said I'd captured the essential Catherine in your portrait, didn't I?' Nik said huskily, and she saw that she was indeed the painting sprung to life.

He turned her to him, tilting her mouth up for his kiss, then, as the embrace deepened and she clung to him, he swung her off the ground to carry her back through to the bedroom. He laid her on

the bed, shed his robe, and as she lifted her arms
to him he came down beside her...

Endless days followed—on the beach, swimming,
sunbathing, playing Nik's peculiar version of beach
tennis, which she always seemed to win. Or riding
about the island on his motorbike, up steep, isolated tracks which wound through the pine trees
and gave glimpses of the sapphire Aegean far below.
They would picnic on bread and cheese, olives and
grapes, enveloped in the spicy, resinous scent of the
trees, then curl up in each other's arms to while
away the dragging heat of afternoon, before riding
slowly back to the villa.

And it seemed so perfectly, marvellously right for
her to be here. All the long eight years had dropped
away, years when she'd been merely waiting for this
time, waiting to complete what had begun when
she was barely more than a child, to make her into
a fulfilled woman.

Each evening after dinner, they walked through
the olive groves, as the falling dusk released the
potent scent of the honeysuckle and brought the
song of the nightingale. And every night they lay
entwined in the meadow, then later in Nik's bed,
seeking one another with a greed which could never
be wholly sated.

Most days, as though by some instinct, they both
woke together, but one morning she roused first
and eased herself up to look at Nik as he lay, his
arms outstretched, a lock of black hair over his

brow. Like this, he looked just as he had that first summer, when he'd slept in the midday heat beneath the pines. But now they lay together, not as friends but as lovers—those days of innocence were gone, but she had gained so much more. And instead of one magical summer, they would go on for ever.

But would they? This summer, too, would end. The flowers in the meadow would fade, and the winds of autumn and the rains of winter would come. 'Let's drink to the present—forget the future.' Well, they had, with an intensity which had altered irrevocably every fibre of her being. And yet... 'Forget the future.' One day, in that future, Nik being the man he was—casual, happy go lucky—would surely turn his back and walk away from her with a final 'See you', just as he had that other time. No, there was no future for her with Nik—and he'd never pretended otherwise, never once mentioned her staying on here once her holiday was over.

Her holiday! In sudden panic, she eased back the sheet and tiptoed across the passage to her own room. Her bag was in the wardrobe; she pulled it out, sat down on the bed and began fumbling through it. Passport, credit cards, traveller's cheques—and flight ticket. With unsteady hands she flipped it open and saw the date—Friday, the twenty-first of May. But what was the date today? What day of the week was it? For, totally absorbed in Nik, it was as though she'd fallen out of Time...

Her watch, which she had not worn for days, lay beside her bed and reaching for it, almost unwillingly, she saw the date—the twentieth of May. And on Monday she must be back at her desk. There was that nine-thirty appointment with—what was he called? Desperately, she flogged her brain, for it seemed somehow imperative that she remember. Ah yes, Mr Russo—she was seeing him about that loan for his new restaurant. She'd done every last iota of the paperwork before she'd left. And now—how laid-back—no, how irresponsible could she be? Clutching the watch in her hand, she sat staring at the opposite wall...

Nik was in the kitchen. When she appeared he smiled across at her, then, not seeming to notice that her heart was quietly breaking, said, 'Make the salad, will you?' and she responded carefully, 'Yes, of course.'

It was a day of blue sky and soft sea breezes which rustled the pines over their heads. Catherine sat, her chin propped on her knees, and thought, with a stab of bitter-sweet pain, I don't believe there has ever been such a perfect, glorious day. Then, feeling Nik's eyes on her behind his sunglasses, she smiled that brilliant smile which had begun to slip, just as he pulled her down beside him, to join him in their private world.

They were back at the villa, sipping iced lemonade on the veranda, when she said abruptly, 'Nik, I-I'm leaving tomorrow.'

'I know that, *agape mou*.' His eyes were expressionless but she saw a tiny muscle tug at the corner of his mouth.

'But how? I mean——'

The faintest smile. 'My little one, I know you so well that I almost catch your thoughts before you think them.'

'In that case——' she made a pathetic attempt at insouciance '—you'll know why I have to go.'

'Of course.'

'Aren't you going to try to dissuade me?'

'Could I?' He quirked a black brow, a hint of the old sardonic Nik in his voice.

'Probably.' She bent forward, her hair tumbling round her face, to stare down at her twining fingers.

Putting down his glass, Nik came over to her and went down on his haunches.

'Catherine——' he took her hands between his, turning them over and softly stroking his thumb across each palm '—you know what I want.'

'Do I?' A sad little smile.

'I want you beside me. I want to wake with you in my arms, sleep again with you in my arms, endlessly lying in the flower meadow, paint you again and again to catch your every mood. But you know the kind of man I am, the kind of life I lead, so—I shall not try to persuade you. And now——' when she did not reply '—we will have a special meal for your last evening.'

Candles, flowers, champagne, she in her pink dress, Nik in a white shirt and dark grey cords. But the candle glow shimmered, the flowers were blurred by the sheen of her tears, and when she sipped the champagne she tasted only the strawberries of that first morning.

At last, Nik put down the coffee spoon which he had been abstractedly playing with for half an hour, took her up in his arms and carried her off to bed. He made love to her with a fierce yet tender passion which shattered her fragile composure, so that when at last he lay asleep, the thick black lashes hiding those sardonic blue-black eyes, the thin mouth relaxed into a tender half-smile, she wept slow, anguished tears into her pillow.

He was not there when she woke. She thought perhaps he'd gone for ever, like last time, but as she closed her case he appeared in the doorway. His face wore that bleak expression which turned the knife in her.

'I've ordered a taxi—it will be here in an hour.' His lips twisted wryly. 'I didn't imagine you'd want to ride to the airport clinging to the back of my motorbike.'

'Th-thank you.'

'I'll get you some breakfast.'

If she tried to eat anything, it would choke her. 'No, thank you—I'm not hungry.'

'Just coffee, then.'

When she went out on to the veranda, he set down a cup and a bowl of fruit.

'I'll leave you to it.' And before she could take his hand, beg him to stay, beg him to beg her to stay, he had gone.

The taxi was early and pulled up on the grass just as Nik appeared with her luggage. He greeted the driver, then opening the car boot, dropped in her case, straightened up and turned to face her.

'I seem to remember promising you this once.' As she stared mutely up at him, he took off his St Christopher and hung it round her neck. 'Your hair's in the way. Turn round.'

She felt his fingers push the tendrils aside, then the clasp was fastened and her hair fell back into place. As she looked down at the small silver medallion, her throat and chest tightened as if an iron fist had clenched on them.

'Catherine.' He took her by the shoulders, his eyes sombre.

'Y-yes, Nik?'

'*Kalo taksithi*—travel safely, little one.'

He brushed her forehead just once with his lips, then opened the rear door, and as she climbed in, closed it again and handed the driver a bank note. As the car moved off down the track, she risked a glance out of the rear window. He was already going back up the steps. Biting her lip, she watched him out of sight, her eyes dry and gritty, but then, turning round, caught the driver's gaze in the mirror and hastily put on her sunglasses.

As the plane levelled off, its wing dipped so that the whole island came suddenly into view. Down there, out past Aselinos Beach, was Nik. Was he in his studio? Was he at this moment standing, brush in hand, listening to the plane? And only then she remembered her portrait, waiting for a rich tourist to take a fancy to it.

She swayed in her seat as a faint moan of anguish was torn from her, then, meeting the concerned stare of the young woman beside her, she turned her face away and closed her eyes.

CHAPTER TEN

'So THERE'S nothing at all for you to worry about, Mrs Hendricks.'

'Yes, thank you, Miss Turner. You've really put my mind at rest.' The middle-aged woman returned Catherine's reassuring smile.

'As soon as I've finalised the figures I'll let you have a formal copy—by Wednesday at the latest.' Catherine stood up and escorted the woman out of her office.

But the bright, professional smile faded even as she closed the door, and she leaned up against it wearily for several seconds before going to sit at her desk again.

A few tendrils of hair had escaped from her smooth chignon and she brushed them back with her hands, then held her palms to her brow to try and ease the tight band which every afternoon now seemed to settle there. She probably needed glasses with all this close work at the computer screen, but somehow it seemed too much trouble to make an appointment with an optician.

She picked up a pencil and toyed with it. Had she been right to take this job—a sideways move, not promotion, from the London bank to a smaller branch in King's Lynn? She'd told herself that it offered excellent varied experience which would enhance her career prospects. Besides, she knew—and loved—the area, for in her childhood she'd spent many carefree childhood holidays in this part of the Norfolk coast.

So she'd snatched at the chance to get away from the silent reproaches at home, and the never-ending possibility of bumping into Julian. But, even though she hoped it wasn't showing yet, she had to face it—her zest for work, the more the better, her pleasure in making decisions, solving difficult problems—all that had gone.

The phone at her elbow rang and she picked it up.

'Yes, Roseanne, put him through, please. Hello, Philip. Yes,' her glance strayed to a bulging file on her desk, 'I've got it finished—I'll bring it through to you. Oh, and about that rescheduling proposal I spoke to you about—I can let you have that first thing on Monday... No, not at all. I can work at it over the weekend... No, honestly, I'll be glad to.'

The side street which led down to the river and docks area of the town was an oasis of quiet after the Friday evening rush hour mêlée. She walked slowly upstairs to her third-floor flat, let herself in, then closed the door. The end of another week. She needn't see a soul until Monday morning if she didn't want to—unless she went shopping in the morning and forced herself finally to a decision over her sitting-room carpet. Should it be the pale green Wilton, or that off-white shag-pile?

Just thinking about it made her headache worse. She kicked off her shoes, took a couple of painkillers, then made herself a pot of tea and a couple of rounds of toast—what was becoming more and more her usual evening meal—and sat down in front of the early evening TV news. But when that seemed even more unbearable than usual, she moved her chair over to the big bay window.

At the end of the street a smart wine bar had opened a few days ago, and as she gazed out she could see people arriving from work for a reviving drink. A young couple, their arms round each other's waists, paused on the pavement for a long, long kiss, then as Catherine watched they disappeared through the olive green and gilt front door.

Just for a moment, she had the crazy urge to dress up, run downstairs and join them all. For surely what was wrong with her was that she was turning into a recluse. Soon after her arrival, two of her fellow employees had asked her for a date, but she'd refused each so peremptorily that both young men had treated her warily ever since.

Some time in the night, as usual, she woke very suddenly, her mouth dry, her heart pounding, from the dream. Very often it was there in the daytime as well, but then she blotted it out super-efficiently. At night, though, she had no defence. Tonight, as always, she was lying in the meadow, among the flowers, and Nik was bending towards her, to take her in his arms and—— With a groan, Catherine rolled over, pressing her face into the pillow in a vain attempt to blot out the images...

She got up very early, heavy-eyed from lack of sleep, and made a pot of coffee. The rescheduling file sat on the side table, the old worn carpet square stared reproachfully up at her, but all at once she couldn't stay in the silent flat a second longer. She dressed, pulling on jeans, trainers, a royal blue fleecy sweatshirt, then stared at herself in the mirror. Once upon a time, she never had casual, easy-going items like this in her wardrobe. Her lips tightened, and she turned away, snatched up her bag, and ran downstairs.

As she drove off, the postman was making his way down the street and she slowed momentarily. But why should today be any different, when there'd been nothing—not a single word—for over three months now? In fact, the only letter she'd had from Greece was from Mr Joannides, acknowledging without comment her own letter renouncing any claim to the villa, but adding, in his usual cryptic fashion, that certain 'complications' had recently arisen concerning the matter.

At Holme-next-the-Sea she parked in the little field which served as a car park. Slipping on her pink mohair jacket—it was only the last week in August, but out here on the eastern edge of England the wind already had a crisp autumn bite—she walked through the dunes, her heart lifting, in spite of the misery inside her, at the first sight of the expanse of pale golden beach and surging green water.

Every summer she'd held her breath, waiting for this view, terrified that it might somehow have vanished. She could see herself, a rather solemn little girl with tight blonde plaits, in a neat white dress and ankle socks, clutching a bucket and spade.

She walked for an hour or more along the tideline, almost oblivious of the seabirds wheeling overhead. Then, just at her feet, she saw a large winkle shell and stooped to pick it up. Usually they were broken, but this one was quite perfect, and, sitting down on a patch of dry sand, she turned it over and over in her hands.

One morning, Gramps had opened that old cabinet of his and shown her his collection of conch shells. 'If you hold one to your ear, you can hear the sea,' he'd said...

Lifting the shell to her ear, she closed her eyes. Instantly, above the sound of the Norfolk sea, she heard the soft shush of waves breaking gently on to a Greek shore, and she saw two figures lying at the water's edge, entwined in each other's arms.

And, quite suddenly, she knew the truth. She'd come here, to Norfolk, trying to recapture an earlier, safer time, before she'd ever met Nik, before the agonies of a broken heart. But it was no use. She could run away from him—she could run to the corners of the earth, but he had invaded her whole being. She loved him, and she was pining, wasting away for him. In leaving him, she'd sought security, which was what she'd thought she yearned for above everything else. And she had that security now—but it lay in ruins around her.

She got to her feet and, stumbling in the soft, yielding sand, began to run back to her car.

The taxi dropped her at the bottom of the hill. She picked up her overnight bag and began walking, still rehearsing what she would say.

But supposing he wasn't alone? The terrible thought jolted her stomach. You're a fool, do you know that? He just isn't the kind of man to stay alone for long. What will you do if there's another woman with him—if Elena's there, with her voluptuous, *sated* body?

She halted, sweat making her hold on the case slip, and for a moment she thought of turning and running. But no—she'd run away last time, hadn't she, because she wasn't brave enough to face the truth—and she went on up the track.

There was no one at the villa. The door was locked, all the shutters were barred, and a spider had constructed an intricate web across one of them, while some dead leaves lay scattered across the veranda. Nik hadn't been here for weeks— maybe the whole summer.

Tears scorched her eyes at the thought of the villa lying neglected, but then, on an impulse, she went over to the terracotta pot. He wouldn't have left it, of course—— Almost disbelievingly, she brought out the key and crouched, staring at it. Then very slowly she straightened up, let herself in, and dropping her case in the kitchen, went through the house, opening every door.

The studio was just as it had been—there was even a faint smell of paint and linseed, though there was nothing of that elusive sandalwood which was Nik himself. All the paintings of Elena were there; only her own portrait had gone from the easel. So he'd done what he'd threatened—sold it.

Her face screwed up with pain and, turning quickly away, she went into his bedroom. Here, everywhere was tidy, the bed—she forced herself to look down at it—was stripped, but in the far corner of the wardrobe lay an old black T-shirt. As she stooped to take it out, the fatigue, on top of the unhappiness of many weeks, made her sway unsteadily and her legs almost gave way. She couldn't sleep here though—not in this room, not on that bed, where she and Nik—— She bit her lip, then, going to her own darkly shuttered room, curled up on the bare mattress.

Nik would soon know she was here—he probably knew already. If he wanted to come—if it wasn't too late—he would. Cradling the shirt to her, she plunged headlong into a deep, dreamless sleep...

He came next morning. She had slept for over twelve hours, then woken, showered, put on a cream Indian muslin sundress and gone out on to the veranda, just as he walked up the path.

She stopped at the top of the steps as he arrived at the bottom, and they looked at one another in silence. He was wearing a blue denim suit, the jacket slung casually over one shoulder. He looked tired and his face was thinner. She just had time to register that before, with no carefully rehearsed little speech, nothing except, 'Hello, Nik, I've come back,' she went down the steps and into his arms.

He held her close, his face buried in her hair, but at last he pushed her gently to arm's length, looking down at her as though searching her face.

'Tell me why you've come, Catherine.'

The intensity of his gaze burned into her, but she met it squarely. 'I've come back, Nik, because I love you.' And when he did not respond, she went on, 'I know now that my life is empty without you.'

'But *with* me—it might be such a precarious life. Could you face that, Catherine—the insecurity, year after year, maybe?' He sounded almost stern.

'I only know that I can't l-live without you.' She gave him an uncertain smile. 'I'm being very forward, aren't I? You've never told me that you love *me*.'

But still he made no response, so, running the tip of her tongue round her dry lips, she forced herself rapidly on. 'I went back to England because I was afraid. It was like a dream here—I wanted to stay so very much, but part of me threw up its oh, so respectable hands in horror at the idea of spending the rest of its days with a struggling, *irresponsible* artist.'

'Instead of enjoying the life provided by an up and coming bank manager?' There was just a hint of that irrepressible gleam of irony in his eyes, before he went on, 'But you've come back.'

'Yes,' she said simply, 'to take whatever comes, and be happy just to have you. That is——' her voice faltered '—if you still want me. Perhaps you——'

'Oh, my little love.' Nik caught both her hands. 'Forgive me,' he said huskily. 'If you only knew what it cost me to let you go that terrible day——' his grip tightened until she almost cried out with the pain '—seeing you go, not knowing if you would ever come back—loving you as I did.'

'L-loving me?'

'My darling girl, I think I've loved you since you were sixteen.' A wry little grimace. 'Even though it took me eight years to discover that.'

'And me too,' she put in softly. 'But now—I think I've finally grown up.'

He gave her a smile that made every pulse in her leap with joy. 'Into a woman more lovely, more desirable than I could ever have imagined. My dear love,' a shaky laugh, 'don't ever leave me again. The waiting has almost killed me, even though I knew that you had to be free to make your own decision. I'm a very patient man——'

'Really?' She looked up at him from beneath demure lashes.

'Yes, really,' he growled. 'But a hundred times I have been on the verge of flying to England, to snatch you up and carry you off—by force, if necessary.'

'Mmmm, that would have been nice,' she whispered dreamily.

'I'd have come to King's Lynn and——'

'King's Lynn?' The dreamy gaze turned to wide-eyed astonishment.

'Oh, yes. I have—contacts in England, who have kept me informed.'

'But, why?'

'Well,' a slanted look, 'it may not have occurred to you, but the way we were behaving, you could well have been pregnant.'

'Oh.' Catherine blushed rose-pink. 'I shouldn't have minded,' she murmured.

'Well, I would,' he said brusquely. 'I'd have insisted on taking care of you, of course, but I want our first child to be born in wedlock.'

'Wedlock! You mean——?'

'But, of course. Oh, *khartpenos, agapenos, kharthea mou.*'

'What does that mean?'

'My darling, my love, my heart.'

'*Khartpenos, agapenos, kharthea mou,*' she repeated hesitantly. 'Is that right?'

'Perfect.' His smile melted her insides, but then his eyes grew serious again. 'And you are prepared to take me on—to marry me?'

'Oh, yes, Nik.' Happiness was flooding her parched heart like soft golden rain.

'And if the seam of rich tourists should ever run dry?'

'Well, we'll just have to survive on bread and cheese. Or maybe we could pawn that watch of yours.' She gave him a sideways look.

'Or that bracelet of yours.' He took the arm that was wearing it, pressing his lips to the inner wrist. 'Or your St Christopher, perhaps?'

'No—never.' She laid her hand on her throat protectively and he laughed.

'Well—maybe neither sacrifice will be necessary.' But then the laughter faded, and his eyes went very dark. 'Catherine.'

Pulling her roughly into his arms, he kissed her with a sudden fierceness which made her cling to him. Just as abruptly, though, he thrust her away from him with a groan.

'I feel like a man who's been starving for months, then sees a table full of delicacies placed in front of him.'

'Well, then——' she lifted her arms slightly '—I'm here.'

'*No.*' He gave her a mock scowl. 'I won't lay a finger on you until we're married. I suppose you'll want a big wedding in England?'

'No,' she said simply. 'I just want you.'

He laughed triumphantly. 'Then we'll be married in Athens on—what's today, Tuesday?—on Friday.'

'Oh, yes, please, Nik.' The dizziness was sweeping through her again.

'But until then,' he shook his finger in stern admonishment, 'you are under my protection. Which is why I am taking you to my parents' apartment in Athens—now.'

She gaped at him. Whatever had happened to that indolent, laid-back Nik?

'Where's your luggage? I was told you brought one case.'

'You were——? Oh, don't tell me—the Skiathos bush telegraph at work.'

'But of course,' he agreed suavely. 'Another old schoolfriend—he works in immigration control.'

'I should have known.' She laughed. 'I seem to remember asking you once if there was anything at all you didn't know about me. I didn't realise then that I was up against the entire Skiathos old boys' network.'

'And I seem to remember saying that I had hardly started to learn about you. And that, my love, is still true—but now we have the rest of our lives, just the two of us, to put that right.'

With a last hug for his plump little mother, Nik steered Catherine along the marble-tiled corridor.

'All right?' He rolled his eyes commiseratingly.

'Yes—they're—very nice,' she replied breathlessly.

They had been swept inside the apartment, in a pleasant, leafy suburb near the old royal palace, on a tide of joyful exclamations. She'd watched as 'Nikolaos' was clutched fervently to his mother's bosom, while his father—an older, grizzled version of Nik—exchanged smiling glances with her, from eyes which were astonishingly like his son's. Then it had been her turn to be embraced, after which they'd gathered round the table for a ceremonial little meal with coffee, pink and white Turkish delight piled in glass dishes with lace doyleys, and baklava cake drenched in honey.

Her luggage was already in the pretty little guest room and at this very moment, she'd gathered, Mrs Demetrios was on the telephone to her dressmaker. The speed of events was almost making her reel, as Nik steered her into one of the lifts.

They got out at the top floor and he ushered her along the corridor, stopping in front of the only door.

'Is this the penthouse?' She looked around her.

'That's right.'

Nik was busy digging out a key from his pocket. He put it in the lock, opened the door and gestured her in ahead of him, through a wide hall lit by a glass dome, and into a huge sitting-room, running the entire width of the block.

It was superbly furnished in a mixture of old and new: modern teak like honey-satin and low-slung cream leather sofas and chairs, side by side with antique pieces and lovely old Chinese washed-silk rugs. On one wall were three paintings, all of them looking extremely genuine.

'Do you like it?' Nik was behind her.

'It's beautiful.'

She walked across to the enormous sliding windows which gave a view over most of Athens, surmounted by the Acropolis like a child's model. When she turned, he was watching her.

'I don't understand,' she said slowly, almost fearfully. 'This apartment——?'

'Is mine.'

'You mean, you *rent* it?'

'Not exactly.' He pulled a face, then coming across to her took her hand and sat her down on one of the cream leather sofas. 'I have a slight confession to make, *agape mou*. You see, I'm not really a painter.'

'But you are—a brilliant one.' She put her arms round him, hugging him. 'You're the best.'

Nik gave her a funny little smile, then tenderly brushed her cheek with his fingertip.

'I didn't exactly mean that. And I don't rent this flat, I own it—and the block.'

'Oh.' Catherine, very pale, stared at him, her hazel eyes almost swallowing the rest of her face.

'And,' he went on, 'you know you told Julian that you could never marry a bank manager?'

'Y-yes.'

'Well,' he paused for a moment, 'how do you feel about marrying the head of one?'

'One what?' she asked stupidly.

'One international merchant bank.'

CHAPTER ELEVEN

'YOU mean—you are——?' She broke off, quite overcome, and he nodded.

'A big one?' she asked faintly.

'One of the biggest, I'm afraid,' he replied gravely, though a wicked imp glinted in his eyes.

'But——' there was a strange little pain at her heart '—why didn't you tell me, Nik?'

'Forgive me, *koukla mou*.' He raised her hand to his lips. 'I didn't intend to deceive you—at least, not at first—but when this affair of the villa began I had seized the chance to take a break—my very first for eight years.'

'Since...?'

'That's right. Ever since that summer, I've given myself over to work—to building up the bank, and making my way within it. My one relaxation was my painting, but even I was beginning to realise that it was time I slowed up. So, I went back to my roots—to Skiathos—where I was just rediscovering what I'd almost forgotten—that there are other things in life to set beside the pursuit of power and wealth. Then you came. You took me for—what was your word?—an "irresponsible artist" and I chose not to disabuse you.'

'But you were selling your paintings in that gallery.'

'Not so much *that* gallery,' he almost looked guilty, 'as mine. I own that as well.'

'I see.' She looked down, picking at a loose thread in her dress, then back up to him. 'But why, Nik?'

'Please try to understand, my sweet. Even though, from the very first moment I saw you again, I was a lost man, I had to be sure of you.' He took her hand once more. 'You seemed so intent on gaining material security—all the things that Julian could offer—that I knew that if I won you from him, it had to be for myself alone.'

'It's true. I *was* shallow—I see that now. But poor Julian—he didn't stand a chance,' she said ruefully.

'Poor Julian?' He pulled a wry face. 'When he arrived, I was terrified of him.'

'So that's why you were so awful to him.' She gave him a glimmering smile. 'But there was no need. I was already head over heels in love with you—even if I didn't realise it till afterwards.'

'So, now that you know the truth, do you think you can break your resolution never to marry a banker?'

'Well, I'll have to think about it. I'm not really——' she began provokingly, but as Nik seized her round the waist she gave a squeak. 'Yes—yes! I think I just might be able to make an exception in your case.'

'Oh, my little love!'

Nik kissed her then drew her into his arms and held her close, so that she could feel his heart beating against her breast. They sat motionless for several minutes, wrapped round in happiness, before Nik stirred. He glanced at the marble clock on the mantelshelf and pulled a face.

'Darling, forgive me, but I have a very important meeting which I can't break, not even for you. Representatives of a Tokyo bank are waiting to see me—I'd have put them off but I only heard that you were here when I got back from the States this morning and they had arrived by then. But afterwards, I'll buy you your engagement ring—and our wedding rings, of course. Now, come and help me change.'

Pulling her to her feet, he towed her into his bedroom, attractively furnished in earthy, masculine shades. But it was not the glowing Afghan carpets which took her eye, or the amber silk coverlet on the bed, but the portrait hanging opposite. She turned to Nik, her eyes very bright.

'You didn't really think I'd sell it, did you?' he said softly. 'My angel—I needed that to keep me company through the long months of waiting.'

Then, as if to rupture the slightly sombre mood, he threw back a wall-length wardrobe door.

'You can choose my clothes. You have such superb taste in everything—especially husbands. Ouch!' He rode her punch at his midriff. 'Now, what do you think?'

'Well,' lips pursed, she scanned the formidable array, 'a white silk shirt, I think. And this suit.' She took out a pale grey one. 'But which tie?' She ran her hands slowly along thirty beautiful silk ties.

Nik laughed. 'You decide, while I shower.'

Kicking off his shoes and socks, he slung his denim jacket across the bed then peeled off his shirt and unzipped his trousers. He stepped out of them, so that he was wearing only navy briefs, which were slung low on his narrow hips.

Catherine stood there, devouring him, her eyes darkening with desire.

'Oh, Nik, what are you trying to do to me?' she asked in a throaty whisper.

He gave her a crooked smile. 'Just trying to make you as crazy for me as I am for you.'

Taking her in his arms, he held her to him again, burying his face in the angle of her neck, and with a fierce joy she felt the desire quicken in him. But then he thrust her way. 'No, my sweet.'

'I'll come and scrub your back if you like,' she said demurely.

'Sorry,' he dropped a last kiss on her throat, 'but that is something I only allow my wife to do.' And he disappeared into the bathroom.

He looks wonderful, of course, she told herself as she put the finishing touch to the knot of his blue floral silk tie. Funny how she'd once thought that he could never wear anything other than casual old jeans and T-shirts. That had been one Nik. But this new Nik—sleek and smooth, exuding the power and arrogance which only wealth gives—he was hers, as well. Forever.

'Will I do?' He smiled down at her as she handed him his slim-line brief case.

'Very well. But will I?' All at once she was filled with uncertainty.

He tilted her face and studied it, his eyes very intent. 'Oh, yes,' he said softly. 'Yes, my darling.'

'Happy, Kyria Demetrios?'

'Mmmm.' As Nik nuzzled his mouth gently against the side of her neck, she arched it slightly. 'Happy, Kyrie Demetrios?'

She felt him smile against her pulse. 'Perfectly, wonderfully, utterly happy.'

She was lying in his lap in one of the bamboo chairs on the veranda, but now he held her away from him slightly.

'Keep still.' He brushed back her hair, so that several grains of rice fell on to the sleeve of her jade-green silk dress, then he picked one up between his finger and thumb. 'Fertility in marriage—that's what rice means, doesn't it?' he asked casually.

'So I've heard,' she said demurely.

'But what about that job I want you to take on our English desk?'

'Well, we shall just have to see how soon the rice takes effect, shan't we?' She gave him another wide-eyed look, and he caught up her hand, burying his face in the palm.

'Oh, Catherine, I love you so much that it hurts.'

'And I love you so much that—there's nothing left of me apart from that,' she said almost wonderingly.

'And what about your parents?' he asked wryly. 'Do you think that they will come to love me as well?'

'Hmmm.' She pretended to ponder the question. 'I think they're coming round—slowly, of course— to the idea that their new son-in-law is one of the richest men in Greece.' She gave a gurgle of laughter. 'I don't think Mum quite believed it at first—it was that fabulous marble and gold bathroom in their guest suite that finally convinced her. Oh, and this, of course.'

She held up her left hand, the huge flawless diamond sparkling in the sunlight, next to the wide band of plain gold, and their eyes met in the shared memory of that moment when, lost to everything in the church beyond their two selves—the glowing vestments of the priests, the candles, the flowers— he had slid the wedding ring onto her finger.

'And what about *your* parents?'

'Oh—delighted that their master plan succeeded.'

'What plan?'

'My father made a clean breast of it this morning, just before he set out for the church. It seems, *koukla*,' he gave a wry grimace, 'that I'm not the only con artist in the family. We were both set up.'

'But how?'

'The dispute over the villa—there *was* no dispute.'

She gaped at him. 'You mean, the wager—it never happened?'

'No, that took place all right, exactly as we heard. It was just that later, they saw how to make use of it. You remember your grandfather coming to England?'

'Of course.'

'Well, he came back with two pieces of information which he confided to my father. The London clinic had confirmed what he knew in his heart already—that he had, at the most, another year to live.' As Catherine bit her lip, he took her hand and stroked it gently.

'And what was the second thing?' Although she was beginning to guess.

'That that spark of—difference which he'd detected in you was being smothered by your parents and Julian between them. At the same time, my parents were becoming more than a little anxious that I should "settle down", as my mother put it, so they cooked up the row over the villa between them. Your grandfather had, of course, honoured the wager and made a new will, but it was lodged with my father's lawyer in Athens. Stavros Joannides would have been in an impossible position if he'd been party to their little scheme.'

'But how was that going to bring us together? All that we did was fight like cat and dog.'

'Oh, they just hoped that when the fighting stopped, the old chemistry between us would start to do its work again.'

'Again? You mean they knew—about us, last time?'

'Oh yes.' He grinned ruefully. 'Your grandfather was keeping much more of a watchful eye over you—and, more particularly, me—than either of us realised. And, as for my parents, they saw what it's taken me eight years to see, that ever since that day when a lovely young girl came out of the sea towards me, well, there's never been anyone else.'

'Oh, Nik.' The smile shimmered on her face.

'So,' he eased her gently to her feet, 'let's go into our villa, shall we?'

'Mmmm. *Our* villa.' But then, 'Oh, I've just remembered. You know I wrote to Mr Joannides giving up my claim to the house?'

'Yes.'

'Well, he wrote back saying there were complications. Do you know what they are?'

He chuckled. 'I rather think so. You see, the very day your letter arrived, I went to see Stavros to tell him that I was giving up *my* claim.'

'But why?'

He brushed his finger across her lips in a butterfly kiss. 'Because *khartpenos mou*, this house, however beautiful, was an empty shell without you.'

They stood, arms twined, then Catherine said softly, 'Can we go down to the olive grove? It's been so long since I've seen it.'

But then, minutes later, as she looked around her, 'Oh, no, the flowers have all gone.'

'They'll come next year—they always come again. And look.'

Stooping down, he picked one solitary poppy and she took it, gazing down at the fading silk petals the sooty heart.

'You know,' she said softly, 'while I was away every night I dreamed I was here.'

He quirked a teasing brow. 'Oh, and what were you doing?'

She laughed, blushing rosily. 'I'm not sure I should tell you.'

'Maybe some of the same things that I was doing in *my* dreams.' He gave her a slanted smile. 'But now, who needs dreams when we're holding the reality in our arms?'

Lifting her face to his, he looked down at her then murmured something in Greek.

'What does that mean?'

He shook his head. 'You will have to learn my language.'

'Of course,' she responded demurely. 'You can give me my first lesson now.'

'Oh, no, *agape mou*, I have quite another lesson in mind for you tonight.'

Holding her tightly to him as though he would never let her go, he bent his head and kissed her. Their bodies fused, melting into one another as the passion between them ignited, until they fell slowly to their knees, hands and lips searching and discovering, taking and giving.

When the new moon slid up the sky, turning the rustling olive leaves above their heads to silver, neither of them saw it. And when the nightingale began his glorious, haunting melody, he was singing only to himself.

UNLOCK THE DOOR TO GREAT ROMANCE AT BRIDE'S BAY RESORT

Join Harlequin's new across-the-lines series, set in an exclusive hotel on an island off the coast of South Carolina.

Seven of your favorite authors will bring you exciting stories about fascinating heroes and heroines discovering love at Bride's Bay Resort.

Look for these fabulous stories coming to a store near you beginning in January 1996.

Harlequin American Romance #613 in January
Matchmaking Baby by Cathy Gillen Thacker

Harlequin Presents #1794 in February
Indiscretions by Robyn Donald

Harlequin Intrigue #362 in March
Love and Lies by Dawn Stewardson

Harlequin Romance #3404 in April
Make Believe Engagement by Day Leclaire

Harlequin Temptation #588 in May
Stranger in the Night by Roseanne Williams

Harlequin Superromance #695 in June
Married to a Stranger by Connie Bennett

Harlequin Historicals #324 in July
Dulcie's Gift by Ruth Langan

Visit Bride's Bay Resort each month wherever Harlequin books are sold.

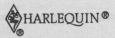

Take 4 bestselling love stories FREE

Plus get a FREE surprise gift!

You're About to Become a *Privileged Woman*

Reap the rewards of fabulous free gifts and benefits with proofs-of-purchase from Harlequin and Silhouette books

Pages & Privileges™

It's our way of thanking you for buying our books at your favorite retail stores.

Harlequin and Silhouette—
the most privileged readers in the world!

For more information about Harlequin and Silhouette's PAGES & PRIVILEGES program call the Pages & Privileges Benefits Desk: 1-503-794-2499

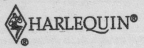

HARLEQUIN®

HP-PP138